序　言

　　教育部專款補助「財團法人語言訓練測驗中心」，推行「全民英語能力分級檢定測驗」後，預計在未來，所有國小、國中學生，以及一般社會人士，如計程車駕駛、百貨業、餐飲業、旅遊業或觀光景點服務人員、維修技術人員、一般行政助理等，均須通過「初級英語能力檢定測驗」，以作為畢業、就業、升遷時之英語能力證明，已是必然趨勢，此項測驗的重要性，可見一斑。

　　繼「初級英語聽力檢定①②」之後，我們再推出「初級英檢模擬試題①②」，完全仿照「初級英語能力檢定測驗」中的題型，書中囊括聽力測驗、閱讀能力測驗，以及寫作能力測驗，希望能幫助讀者輕鬆通過初級檢定的初試測驗。本書試題全部經過劉毅英文「初級英語檢定模考班」，實際在課堂上使用過，效果奇佳。本書所有試題均附有詳細的中文翻譯及單字註解，節省讀者查字典的時間。同時，這些珍貴的試題，也有助於國中同學準備基本學力測驗及第二階段考試。

　　感謝這麼多讀者，給我們鼓勵。編輯好書，是「學習」一貫的宗旨，讀者若需要任何學習英文的書，都可以提供意見給我們，我們的目標是，**學英文的書**，「學習」都有；「**學習**」出版、天天進步。也盼望讀者們不吝給我們批評指正。

編者　謹識

本書製作過程

感謝石支齊老師和張碧紋老師，在試題的收集上，給予很大的幫助，也需感謝劉毅英文「初級英語檢定模考班」的同學們，在上課過程中，提供許多寶貴的意見，讓這些試題更加完善。感謝美籍老師 Laura E. Stewart 負責校訂，也要感謝林惜予小姐協助編寫聽力詳解，以及謝靜芳老師再三仔細校訂，白雪嬌小姐負責封面設計，李佩姍小姐繪製插圖，洪淑娟小姐協助完稿，黃淑貞小姐負責版面設計及打字。

全民英語能力分級檢定測驗
初級測驗①

一、聽力測驗

本測驗分三部份，全為三選一之選擇題，每部份各 10 題，共 30 題，作答時間約 20 分鐘。

第一部份： 看圖辨義

本部份共 10 題，試題冊上每題有一個圖片，請聽錄音機播出一個相關的問題，與 A、B、C 三個英語敘述後，選一個與所看到圖片最相符的答案，並在答案紙上相對的圓圈內塗黑作答。每題播出一遍，問題及選項均不印在試題冊上。

例：（看）

NT$80　　NT$50

（聽）

Look at the picture.　How much is the hamburger?

　　A.　It's eighty dollars.
　　B.　It's fifty-five dollars.
　　C.　It's eighteen dollars.

正確答案為 A

Question 1

Question 2

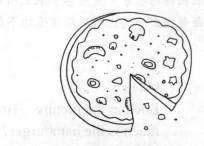

Question 3

Question 4

Question 5

Question 6

請 翻 頁 ⟹

Question 7

Question 8

Question 9

Question 10

請 翻 頁 ⟹

第二部份：問答

本部份共 10 題，每題錄音機會播出一個問句或直述句，
每題播出一次，聽後請從試題冊上 A、B、C 三個選項
中，選出一個最適合的回答或回應，並在答案紙上塗黑
作答。

例：

（聽）　Good morning, Kevin.　How are you?

（看）　A.　I'm fine, thank you.
　　　　B.　I'm in the living room.
　　　　C.　My name is Kevin.

正確答案爲 A

11. A. Last Sunday.
　　B. Two or three times a week.
　　C. I ate out with my classmate.

12. A. Have you been waiting long?
　　B. Yes, it's two o'clock now.
　　C. I'm so sorry I'm late.

13. A. She's our new English teacher.
　　B. She's my niece.
　　C. She's also very smart.

14. A. You'd better get some rest.
　　B. I'll turn on the air conditioner.
　　C. It should be sunny tomorrow.

15. A. It's for you.
    B. I'm sorry. It's busy.
    C. Of course. Help yourself.

16. A. Have a good time!
    B. Do you have a toothache?
    C. These pills are good for a backache.

17. A. How lucky you are!
    B. When did you get back?
    C. Where did you go?

18. A. Where is he going?
    B. I thought he was afraid to fly.
    C. What time does his train arrive?

19. A. You should eat more.
    B. Did you have enough candles?
    C. I did, too.

20. A. Yes, I read.
    B. No, I haven't.
    C. What day is today?

請 翻 頁 ◁▭⇒

第三部份：簡短對話

本部份共 10 題，每題錄音機會播出一段對話及一個相關的問題，每題播出兩次，聽後請從試題冊上 A、B、C 三個選項中，選出一個最適合的回答，並在答案紙上塗黑作答。

例：

（聽）(Woman)　Good afternoon, …Mr. Davis?

　　　(Man)　　Yes.　I have an appointment with Dr. Sanders at two o'clock.　My son Tommy has a fever.

　　　(Woman)　Oh, that's too bad.　Well, please have a seat, Mr. Davis.　Dr. Sanders will be right with you.

　　Question:　Where did this conversation take place?

（看）A.　In a post office.

　　　B.　In a restaurant.

　　　C.　In a doctor's office.

　　　正確答案爲 C

21. A. He thinks they are pretty.
    B. He thinks they are too loud.
    C. He thinks they are very grown-up.

22. A. He prefers steak.
    B. He is a vegetarian.
    C. He is a very moody person.

23. A. They had disappeared.
    B. They were not on the chair where he left them.
    C. He wasn't wearing his glasses.

24. A. A new suit.
    B. A dress that will make her look shorter.
    C. A new dress that makes her look thinner.

25. A. The man met the woman in Japan.
    B. The woman returned from Japan a short time ago.
    C. The woman spent a very long vacation in Japan.

26. A. Less than half an hour.
    B. Nearly seven hours.
    C. At 8:00.

27. A. The woman was very rude to him.
    B. The woman is very busy in the kitchen.
    C. The man has been waiting a long time for his meal.

28. A. She will take a bus with the man.
    B. The man will drive her to the mall.
    C. She will walk to the mall on the corner.

請 翻 頁 ⟹

29. A. He has been waiting
       a long time.
    B. He has been waiting
       five minutes.
    C. He has been waiting
       by himself.

30. A. He thinks she has a
       pretty dress.
    B. He thinks she is not as
       pretty as Alice.
    C. He thinks she is the
       prettiest girl he has
       ever seen.

二、閱讀能力測驗

　　本測驗分三部份，全爲四選一之選擇題，共 35 題，作答時間 35 分鐘。

第一部份： 詞彙和結構
　　　　　　本部份共 15 題，每題含一個空格。請就試題冊上 A、B、C、D 四個選項中選出最適合題意的字或詞，標示在答案紙上。

1. I want to listen to some music. Please _____ on the radio.
   A. open
   B. change
   C. turn
   D. make

2. She hurried _____, ran to the bush and looked under it.
   A. to the downstairs
   B. the downstairs
   C. downstairs
   D. out of the downstairs

3. A : Do you smoke?
   B : No, I've just _____.
   A. given it up
   B. given up it
   C. giving them up
   D. giving up them

請 翻 頁 ◀◻◻⟹

4. I haven't finished my homework, and my younger brother hasn't _____.
   A. too
   B. either
   C. so
   D. neither

5. Father tells me that _____ on time is important.
   A. been
   B. be
   C. is
   D. being

6. People often _____ the newspaper for news every day.
   A. look
   B. watch
   C. read
   D. look at

7. Mary is sixteen. She is _____ young _____ drive.
   A. too ; to
   B. so ; that
   C. enough ; to
   D. between ; and

8. I'm not sure _____ it will rain tomorrow or not.
   A. if
   B. whether
   C. because
   D. when

9. MRT systems, _____ "subways," are built to solve pollution problems.

   A. are called

   B. which are called

   C. call

   D. calling

10. _____ dangerous to ride a motorcycle without a helmet. The helmet can protect your head in accidents.

    A. He's

    B. It's

    C. Its

    D. We're

11. Here is a book _____ he likes very much. He has read it many times.

    A. ×

    B. who

    C. in that

    D. in which

12. John looks very old. _____, he is only twenty years old.

    A. By the way

    B. So far

    C. In fact

    D. Right away

請 翻 頁 ◖⟹

13. The _____ in the cartoon "Pokemon" is quite funny.
    A. cancer
    B. factory
    C. answer
    D. dialogue

14. We will _____ her fourteenth birthday by going out to a
    well-known restaurant.
    A. review
    B. celebrate
    C. decorate
    D. surprise

15. Mary was given a lot of _____ when she had her baby.
    A. ponds
    B. presents
    C. parents
    D. programs

第二部份：段落填空

　　本部份共 10 題，包括二個段落，每個段落各含 5 個空格。
請就試題冊上 A、B、C、D 四個選項中選出最適合題意
的字或詞，標示在答案紙上。

Questions 16-20

My junior high school days were really happy ___(16)___,
though a little boring sometimes. We had to take many tests
every day, and the thing ___(17)___ we had to do was study,
study, and study. But it is ___(18)___ that I loved those days.
___(19)___ it was because we only had to think about our studies.
When I become a senior high school student, I'll read many,
many books ___(20)___. I know hard work will make me a great
man one day.

16. A. them
　　B. one
　　C. ones
　　D. it

17. A. which
　　B. who
　　C. where
　　D. in which

18. A. happy
　　B. fun
　　C. interest
　　D. strange

19. A. When
　　B. After
　　C. Perhaps
　　D. If

20. A. I like to
　　B. I'd like to
　　C. I interest
　　D. I like

請 翻 頁 ◖◗⟹

Questions 21-25

The Internet has changed the world a lot. At first, some parents did not like it because they thought it was ___(21)___ for their children. However, since they began to use the Net, they ___(22)___ that some sites are really helpful. The sites even help children to study better. Although the sites ___(23)___ are most interesting to children are ___(24)___ with lots of games, parents are not worried anymore. They let their children play some games now. Today, ___(25)___ people find they cannot do without the Net. It will surely become even more popular in the near future.

21. A. not good
    B. good
    C. not strange
    D. strange

22. A. learn
    B. learned
    C. have learned
    D. had learned

23. A. how
    B. where
    C. who
    D. which

24. A. the one
    B. the ones
    C. this
    D. these

25. A. fewer and fewer
    B. many and many
    C. less and less
    D. more and more

第三部份： 閱讀理解

本部份共 10 題，包括數段短文，每段短文後有 1～3 個相關問題，請就試題冊上 A、B、C、D 四個選項中選出最適合者，標示在答案紙上。

Questions 26-27

2002 Summer Dances
Parties for Junior High School Students Only

Date : Saturday, June 29
　　　　Sunday, July 28
　　　　Saturday, August 31
Place : Taipei Youth School
Time : 18:00 to 21:00
Cost : NT$300 Each
Tel   : (02) 2383-4949

Bring your friends and get a secret present!

---

26. The parties are held _____.

　　A. for two hours 　　　　　B. every week

　　C. on weekends 　　　　　D. in spring and summer

27. Which is true?

　　A. Anyone who goes to the party can get a present.

　　B. You should go to the party by yourself.

　　C. You have to pay four hundred dollars to go to each party.

　　D. Taipei Youth School will hold three parties this summer.

請翻頁 ►

Questions 28-29

In the United States, it's usual to leave your waiter a tip—extra money for service. Before leaving the restaurant, you leave the tip on the table. Most people leave about 15% of the total bill. Look at Robert's check. Then answer the questions.

hamburger		2.15
fried chicken		4.15
	Tax	0.70
	Total	7.00

28. Robert has to pay $ _____.

 A. 6.30

 B. 7.90

 C. 7.00

 D. 6.75

29. Robert is probably going to leave a tip of $ _____.

 A. 0.33

 B. 0.69

 C. 1.05

 D. 1.50

Questions 30-31

Have you ever wanted to write a song? Two sisters, Mildred and Patty Hill, once <u>composed</u> a little song. It was a happy song that they loved to sing. It was called "Good Morning to You." However, most other people didn't know the song very well.

One day, Mildred and Patty had an idea. It turned out to be a very good idea. They decided to change the words of the song. They called the new song "Happy Birthday to You."

Their short birthday song is now very famous. Almost everyone knows the words. Did anyone sing it at your last birthday?

30. The best title is _____.
    A. How a Famous Song Was Written
    B. Good Morning to You
    C. Why People Like to Sing
    D. Everyone Has a Birthday

31. The word "composed" in line two means _____.
    A. lost
    B. told
    C. wrote
    D. forgot

請 翻 頁 ◀▢⟹

Questions 32-33

The hummingbird is an amazing animal! It can actually flap its wings back and forth seventy-five times a second! This fast movement helps the hummingbird stay in midair while feeding from flowers. Its wings move so fast that they look like a blur.

Not only is the hummingbird fast, but it is also very small, often measuring only two or four inches in length. Hummingbird babies are usually not much bigger than bumblebees.

Although hummingbirds are very small, they are not weak. They have <u>adapted</u> to many different kinds of climates. These little birds can be found all over the Americas—from the southern tip of South America to the lands of the Arctic.

32. The best title is _____.
    A. Birds that Live in Many Lands
    B. The Amazing Hummingbird
    C. Hummingbirds' Wings
    D. Tiny Birds

33. The word "adapted" in line ten means _____.
    A. laid eggs
    B. changed to fit
    C. failed to change
    D. changed colors

Questions 34-35

The street lamps are shaped like chocolate candy "Kisses." The streets have names like East Chocolate Avenue. You are in Chocolate Town, U.S.A. Its real name is Hershey, Pennsylvania.

In 1905, a man named Milton Hershey opened a chocolate factory in a cornfield. Today there are thousands of people living in the town. Visitors are amazed at the huge <u>vats</u> that hold ten thousand pounds of chocolate each. It takes milk from fifty thousand cows every day to help make the candy. There are barns holding 90 million pounds of cacao beans. Chocolate is made from cacao beans.

If you are ever near Hershey, Pennsylvania, stop at the world's largest chocolate factory. There are free samples, too!

34. The word "vats" in line seven means _____.
    A. people
    B. beans
    C. cups
    D. tanks

35. From the size of the factory, you can tell that people like

    _____.
    A. milk
    B. cacao beans
    C. chocolate
    D. visitors

請 翻 頁 ▯⫻⟹

三、寫作能力測驗

　　本測驗共有兩部份，第一部份為單句寫作，第二部份為段落寫作。測驗時間為 40 分鐘。

第一部份：單句寫作

　　　　　請將答案寫在寫作能力測驗答案紙對應的題號旁，如有拼字、標點、大小寫之錯誤，將予扣分。

第 1～5 題：句子改寫

　　　　　請依題目之提示，將原句改寫成指定型式，並將改寫的句子完整地寫在答案紙上（包括提示之文字及標點符號）。

1. Swimming in the river is dangerous.

　　It's ＿＿＿＿＿＿＿＿＿＿＿＿＿＿＿＿＿＿＿＿.

2. I got someone to mail the letter yesterday.

　　I had ＿＿＿＿＿＿＿＿＿＿＿＿＿＿＿＿＿＿＿.

3. You enjoy roller-skating, and he does, too.

　　Not only ＿＿＿＿＿＿＿＿＿＿＿＿＿＿＿＿＿.

4. Every time she comes, she must bring a present to us.

　　She never comes ＿＿＿＿＿＿＿＿＿＿＿＿＿＿.

5. Where is the nearest police station?

　　Tell me ＿＿＿＿＿＿＿＿＿＿＿＿＿＿＿＿＿＿.

第 6～10 題：句子合併

　　　　請依照題目指示，將兩句合併成一句，並將合併的句子
　　　　完整地寫在答案紙上（包括提示之文字及標點符號）。

6. My father painted the house.

   I helped my father.

   _____.

7. I'm talking about that stranger.

   That stranger is wearing a red sweater.（用 in 合併）

   _____.

8. Mr. Lin invited the woman.

   The woman is not very tall.（用 who 合併）

   _____.

9. Linda looks very funny.

   Linda wears that cowboy hat.（用 if 合併）

   _____.

10. Miss White moved the heavy box.

    No one helped her with it.（用反身代名詞合併）

    _____.

請翻頁 ▌⟹

第 11～15 題：重組

　　請將題目中所有提示字詞整合成一有意義的句子，並
將重組的句子完整地寫在答案紙上（包括提示之文字
及標點符號）。答案中必須使用所有提示字詞，且不
能隨意增加字詞，否則不予計分。

11. Ronald's _____.
　　been / away / several times / has / car / towed

12. It's _____.
　　others / wrong / copy / your answers / to let

13. Judy _____.
　　to / be / too / is / on the school / short / basketball team

14. The question _____.
　　children / answer it / that / is / hard / can't / so

15. People _____.
　　water / might / their health / afraid / that / are / harm /
pollution

第二部份：段落寫作

題目：這是妳／你一天的生活，請根據圖片內容寫一篇約50字的
　　　簡短描述。

初級英檢模擬試題①詳解

一、聽力測驗

第一部份

Look at the picture for question 1.

1. (**C**) What is the man doing?

  A. The man is eating food.

  B. The man is looking for food.

  C. The man is cooking food.

  * *look for* 尋找 cook〔kʊk〕v. 煮

Look at the picture for question 2.

2. (**C**) What happened to the pie?

  A. The pie has been eaten.

  B. The pie has been cut into slices.

  C. A piece of the pie has been cut.

  * happen〔'hæpən〕v. 發生 pie〔paɪ〕n. 派

  cut〔kʌt〕v. 切（三態同形） *be cut into* 被切成

  slice〔slaɪs〕n. 薄片 *a piece of* 一片

Look at the picture for question 3.

3. (**A**) What is the man doing?

  A. He is fixing the car.

  B. He is picking up a tool.

  C. He is washing the car.

  * fix〔fɪks〕v. 修理 *pick up* 拿起

  tool〔tul〕n. 工具 wash〔wɑʃ〕v. 洗

Look at the picture for question 4.

4. (**B**) Who is the woman?

    A. She is playing the trumpet.

    B. She is a musician.

    C. She is blowing into a tube.

* trumpet (ˈtrʌmpɪt) *n.* 喇叭
musician (mjuˈzɪʃən) *n.* 音樂家
blow (blo) *v.* 吹   tube (tjub) *n.* 管子

Look at the picture for question 5.

5. (**A**) What is the woman doing?

    A. The woman is buying fish.

    B. The woman is buying fruit.

    C. The woman is buying vegetables.

* fruit (frut) *n.* 水果
vegetable (ˈvɛdʒətəbḷ) *n.* 蔬菜

Look at the picture for question 6.

6. (**C**) What are these children doing?

    A. The children are drinking water.

    B. The children are swimming in the pool.

    C. The children are playing in the water fountain.

* swim (swɪm) *v.* 游泳
pool (pul) *n.* 游泳池 (= *swimming pool*)
fountain (ˈfaʊntṇ) *n.* 噴水池 (= *water fountain*)

Look at the picture for question 7.

7. (**B**) Where are they?

      A. They are on the cloud.

      B. They are in the mountains.

      C. They are in a valley.

      * cloud〔klaʊd〕*n.* 雲　　*in the mountains*　在山中

      valley〔ˈvælɪ〕*n.* 山谷

Look at the picture for question 8.

8. (**B**) What is the woman doing?

      A. She is making coffee.

      B. She is making copies.

      C. She is coughing.

      * *make coffee*　泡咖啡　　copy〔ˈkɑpɪ〕*n.* 影本

      make copies　影印　　cough〔kɔf〕*v.* 咳嗽

Look at the picture for question 9.

9. (**A**) What is true about the picture?

      A. The man is drinking beer.

      B. The woman is wearing a hat.

      C. The man has no money.

      * beer〔bɪr〕*n.* 啤酒　　wear〔wɛr〕*v.* 穿；戴

      hat〔hæt〕*n.* 帽子

Look at the picture for question 10.

10. (**A**) What happened?

    A. The tire needs air.

    B. The car is broken.

    C. The man is fixing his motorcycle.

    * tire〔taɪr〕*n.* 輪胎　　air〔ɛr〕*n.* 空氣

    broken〔'brokṇ〕*adj.* 故障的　　fix〔fɪks〕*v.* 修理

    motorcycle〔'motɚˌsaɪkḷ〕*n.* 摩托車

第二部份

11. (**B**) How often do you eat out?

    A. Last Sunday.

    B. Two or three times a week.

    C. I ate out with my classmate.

    * *How often ~ ?* ～多久一次？（問「頻率」）

    eat out 外出用餐（= *dine out*）　　time〔taɪm〕*n.* 次數

    classmate〔'klæsˌmet〕*n.* 同班同學

12. (**C**) I've been waiting for you for two hours!

    A. Have you been waiting long?

    B. Yes, it's two o'clock now.

    C. I'm so sorry I'm late.

    * *wait for* 等待　　hour〔aʊr〕*n.* 小時

    late〔let〕*adj.* 遲到的

13. (**B**) Who is that cute little girl?

    A. She's our new English teacher.

    B. She's my niece.

    C. She's also very smart.

    * cute〔kjut〕*adj.* 可愛的

       niece〔nis〕*n.* 姪女；外甥女

       smart〔smɑrt〕*adj.* 聰明的

14. (**A**) I think I have a cold.

    A. You'd better get some rest.

    B. I'll turn on the air conditioner.

    C. It should be sunny tomorrow.

    * **have a cold** 感冒（= *catch a cold*）

       had better + *V.* 最好～   rest〔rɛst〕*n.* 休息

       turn on 打開（電器）   **air conditioner** 冷氣

       sunny〔'sʌnɪ〕*adj.* 陽光普照的

15. (**C**) May I use your telephone?

    A. It's for you.

    B. I'm sorry. It's busy.

    C. Of course. Help yourself.

    * use〔juz〕*v.* 使用   telephone〔'tɛlə,fon〕*n.* 電話

       busy〔'bɪzɪ〕*adj.*（電話）佔線中的

       Of course. 當然。

       Help yourself. 自行取用。

16. (**B**) I have a dentist's appointment at 3:00.

    A. Have a good time!

    B. Do you have a toothache?

    C. These pills are good for a backache.

    * dentist〔'dɛntɪst〕*n.* 牙醫

    appointment〔ə'pɔɪntmənt〕*n.* 約會

    Have a good time! 玩得愉快！

    toothache〔'tuθ͵ek〕*n.* 牙痛   pill〔pɪl〕*n.* 藥丸

    be good for 對～有益   backache〔'bæk͵ek〕*n.* 背痛

17. (**A**) My family is going abroad during the winter vacation this year.

    A. How lucky you are!

    B. When did you get back?

    C. Where did you go?

    * abroad〔ə'brɔd〕*adv.* 到國外   ***go abroad*** 出國

    during〔'djurɪŋ〕*prep.* 在～期間

    vacation〔ve'keʃen〕*n.* 假期   ***winter vacation*** 寒假

    lucky〔'lʌkɪ〕*adj.* 幸運的   ***get back*** 回來

18. (**C**) I'm going to pick up my brother at the train station.

    A. Where is he going?

    B. I thought he was afraid to fly.

    C. What time does his train arrive?

    * ***pick up*** *sb.* 開車載某人   ***train station*** 火車站

    be afraid + ***to V.*** 害怕   fly〔flaɪ〕*v.* 搭飛機

    arrive〔ə'raɪv〕*v.* 到達

19. (**B**) We had no power at my house after the typhoon.

        A. You should eat more.

        B. Did you have enough candles?

        C. I did, too.

        * power〔ˋpaʊɚ〕n. 電力　typhoon〔taɪˋfun〕n. 颱風
          enough〔əˋnʌf〕adj. 足夠的　candle〔ˋkændl〕n. 蠟燭

20. (**B**) Have you read the newspaper today?

        A. Yes, I read.　　　B. No, I haven't.

        C. What day is today?

第三部份

21. (**B**) M：I have new neighbors. A young family moved in
            next door yesterday.

        W：How old are their children?

        M：They're pretty young, and very noisy!

        W：Don't worry. They'll grow up.

        Question：What does the man think of his neighbors'
               children?

        A. He thinks they are pretty.

        B. He thinks they are too loud.

        C. He thinks they are very grown-up.

        * neighbor〔ˋnebɚ〕n. 鄰居　***move in*** 搬進（新居）
          next door 在隔壁　pretty〔ˋprɪtɪ〕adv. 很　adj. 漂亮的
          noisy〔ˋnɔɪzɪ〕adj. 吵鬧的　worry〔ˋwɝɪ〕v. 擔心
          grow up 長大　***think of*** 認為
          loud〔laʊd〕adj. 大聲的　grown-up〔ˋgronˋʌp〕adj. 成熟的

22. (**A**)　M：I'm hungry.　How about getting something to eat?

　　　W：What are you in the mood for?

　　　M：I'd like to eat a steak.　How about you?

　　　Question：What is true about the man?

　　　A. He prefers steak.　　　B. He is a vegetarian.

　　　C. He is a very moody person.

　　　＊ hungry〔'hʌŋgrɪ〕*adj.* 飢餓的
　　　　How about～? ～如何？（ = *What about～?* ）
　　　　mood〔mud〕*n.* 心情　　***be in the mood for*** 想要
　　　　steak〔stek〕*n.* 牛排　　true〔tru〕*adj.* 眞實的；正確的
　　　　prefer〔prɪ'fɝ〕*v.* 比較喜歡
　　　　vegetarian〔͵vɛdʒə'tɛrɪən〕*n.* 素食者
　　　　moody〔'mudɪ〕*adj.* 喜怒無常的；情緒多變的

23. (**C**)　W：What are you looking for?

　　　M：I'm trying to find my black socks, but they seem
　　　　　to have disappeared.

　　　W：There they are — on the chair.

　　　M：Oh.　I guess I should wear my glasses.

　　　Question：Why couldn't the man find his socks?

　　　A. They had disappeared.

　　　B. They were not on the chair where he left them.

　　　C. He wasn't wearing his glasses.

　　　＊ ***look for*** 尋找　　socks〔saks〕*n. pl.* 短襪
　　　　seem〔sim〕*v.* 似乎　　disappear〔͵dɪsə'pɪr〕*v.* 消失
　　　　guess〔gɛs〕*v.* 猜想　　wear〔wɛr〕*v.* 戴
　　　　glasses〔'glæsɪz〕*n. pl.* 眼鏡　　leave〔liv〕*v.* 遺留

24. (**C**) W: What do you think of this new dress?

M: I don't think it suits you. It makes you look shorter.

W: What about this one?

M: That one makes you look slim and tall.

W: Then I'll buy it.

Question: What does the woman want to buy?

A. A new suit.

B. A dress that will make her look shorter.

C. A new dress that makes her look thinner.

* ***What do you think of~?*** 你認為～怎麼樣？
  dress〔drɛs〕*n.* 洋裝   suit〔sut〕*v.* 適合 *n.* 西裝
  slim〔slɪm〕*adj.* 苗條的   thin〔θɪn〕*adj.* 瘦的

25. (**B**) M: Hey, I haven't seen you for a long time. Where have you been?

W: I went to Japan for a short vacation.

M: I bet that was fun. When did you get back?

W: Two days ago.

Question: Which of the following is true?

A. The man met the woman in Japan.

B. The woman returned from Japan a short time ago.

C. The woman spent a very long vacation in Japan.

* ***for a long time*** 很久一段時間
  Japan〔dʒə'pæn〕*n.* 日本   ***I bet~*** 我打賭；我肯定
  fun〔fʌn〕*adj.* 好玩的   following〔'faləwɪŋ〕*adj.* 下列的
  return〔rɪ'tɝn〕*v.* 返回

26. (**A**) W：Hurry up, or we're going to be late!

M：What time does the show start?

W：At 8:00, and it's nearly 7:30 now.

M：Relax. We have plenty of time.

Question：How long will it take them to get to the show?

A. Less than half an hour.

B. Nearly seven hours.

C. At 8:00.

* ***hurry up*** 趕快   or〔ɔr〕*conj.* 否則
   show〔ʃo〕*n.* 表演   nearly〔'nɪrlɪ〕*adv.* 將近 (= *almost*)
   relax〔rɪ'læks〕*v.* 放鬆   ***plenty of*** 許多的 (= *a lot of*)
   get to 到達   ***half an hour*** 半小時 (= *a half hour*)

27. (**C**) M：Excuse me, Miss. How long will it be before we get our order?

W：It will be a few more minutes.

M：But we've been waiting nearly 20 minutes already!

W：I'm sorry. They're very busy in the kitchen right now.

Question：Why is the man upset?

A. The woman was very rude to him.

B. The woman is very busy in the kitchen.

C. The man has been waiting a long time for his meal.

* order〔'ɔrdɚ〕*n.* 點餐   minute〔'mɪnɪt〕*n.* 分鐘
   right now 現在   upset〔ʌp'sɛt〕*adj.* 不高興的
   rude〔rud〕*adj.* 無禮的   meal〔mil〕*n.* (一)餐

28. (**B**)　W：Do you know how to get to the new shopping mall?

M：Yes, you have to take a bus from that corner.　But I'm going there now.　I can give you a ride.

W：Thank you very much!

Question：How will the woman get to the shopping mall?

A. She will take a bus with the man.

B. The man will drive her to the mall.

C. She will walk to the mall on the corner.

* **shopping mall** 購物中心（ = *mall* ）

corner〔ˈkɔrnɚ〕*n.* 轉角

give *sb.* **a ride** 讓某人搭便車（ = *give sb. a lift* ）

drive〔draɪv〕*v.* 開車載送某人

29. (**B**)　W：I'm so sorry I'm late.　Have you been waiting a long time?

M：No.　I just got here five minutes ago myself.

Question：How long has the man been waiting?

A. He has been waiting a long time.

B. He has been waiting five minutes.

C. He has been waiting by himself.

* **get here** 到這裏　　**five minutes ago** 五分鐘前

by *oneself* 獨自（ = *alone* ）

30. (**B**) M：Who is that girl in the yellow dress?

W：She's John's sister. She's very pretty, isn't she?

M：She's OK. But I think Alice is prettier.

Question：What does the man think of the girl?

A. He thinks she has a pretty dress.

B. He thinks she is not as pretty as Alice.

C. He thinks she is the prettiest girl he has ever seen.

* *as…as~* 像~一樣…

二、閱讀能力測驗

第一部份：詞彙和結構

1. (**C**) I want to listen to some music. Please <u>turn</u> on the radio.

我想聽點音樂。請<u>打開</u>收音機。

電器的開啟，用 *turn on*，而不是 open。

cf. turn off 關掉（電器）

* *listen to* 聽　　music〔'mjuzɪk〕*n.* 音樂

radio〔'redɪ,o〕*n.* 收音機

2. (**C**) She hurried <u>downstairs</u>, ran to the bush and looked under it.

她趕緊<u>下樓</u>，跑到灌木叢那邊，然後往下看。

依句意，選(C) *downstairs*〔'daʊn'stɛrz〕*adv.* 到樓下

修飾動詞 hurried。

* hurry〔'hɝɪ〕*v.* 匆忙　　bush〔bʊʃ〕*n.* 灌木叢

3. (**A**)　A：Do you smoke?

　　　　　B：No, I've just <u>given it up</u>.

　　　　甲：你抽煙嗎？

　　　　乙：沒有，我才剛戒煙。

　　　　　按照句意爲現在完成式，即「have + p.p.」的動詞時態，
　　　　　故 (C) (D) 不合。give up（戒除）爲可分動詞片語，故
　　　　　「戒煙」有三種寫法：

　　　　　⎧　give up *smoking*　（名詞可置於介系詞後面）
　　　　　⎨　give *smoking* up　（名詞可置於動詞與介系詞中間）
　　　　　⎩　give *it* up　（代名詞只能置於動詞與介系詞中間）

　　　　＊ smoke〔smok〕*v.* 抽煙　　just〔dʒʌst〕*adv.* 剛剛

4. (**B**)　I haven't finished my homework, and my younger
　　　　　brother hasn't <u>either</u>.

　　　　我還沒做完功課，我弟弟也還沒。

　　　　　否定句的「也」置於句尾，用 *either*。

　　　　　⎧　…and my younger brother has*n't, either*.
　　　　　⎨　= …and *neither* has my younger brother.
　　　　　　　（主詞與助動詞須倒裝）

　　　　＊ finish〔ˈfɪnɪʃ〕*v.* 完成

5. (**D**)　Father tells me that <u>being</u> on time is important.

　　　　爸爸告訴我，準時很重要。

　　　　　that 引導的名詞子句中，須填入主詞，而動詞須改爲
　　　　　動名詞或不定詞，才能做主詞，故選 (D) *being*。

　　　　＊ *on time* 準時　　important〔ɪmˈpɔrtn̩t〕*adj.* 重要的

6. (**C**) People often <u>read</u> the newspaper for news every day.

人們通常每天都看報紙以了解新聞。

「看」報紙，動詞用 ***read***。

* news〔njuz〕*n.* 新聞；消息

7. (**A**) Mary is sixteen. She is <u>too</u> young <u>to</u> drive.

瑪麗現年十六歲。她年紀<u>太</u>小，所以還<u>不能</u>開車。

too…to V. 太…以致於不（表否定）

本句可改爲：She is *so* young *that* she can't drive.

* drive〔draɪv〕*v.* 開車

8. (**B**) I'm not sure <u>whether</u> it will rain tomorrow or not.

我不確定明天<u>是否</u>會下雨。

whether…or not 是否（ *= whether = if* ）

* sure〔ʃur〕*adj.* 確定的

9. (**B**) MRT systems, <u>which are called</u> "subways," are built to solve pollution problems.

大衆捷運系統，又<u>名爲</u>「地下鐵」，是爲了解決污染問題而興建的。

空格須填一形容詞子句，且按照句意，「被」稱作地下鐵，須用被動語態，即「be 動詞 + p.p.」的形式。

* ***MRT*** 大衆捷運系統（ *= Mass Rapid Transit* ）
  system〔'sɪstəm〕*n.* 系統　　call〔kɔl〕*v.* 稱爲
  subway〔'sʌb,we〕*n.* 地下鐵　　build〔bɪld〕*v.* 興建
  solve〔salv〕*v.* 解決　　pollution〔pə'luʃən〕*n.* 污染
  problem〔'prabləm〕*n.* 問題

10. (**B**) It's dangerous to ride a motorcycle without a helmet. The helmet can protect your head in accidents.

騎機車不戴安全帽，是件危險的事情。意外發生時，安全帽能保護你的頭部。

虛主詞 It，代替不定詞片語 to ride a motorcycle without a helmet，擺在句首。It is 的縮寫是 **It's**。而 (C) its 是 it 的所有格，用法不合。

* dangerous〔ˈdɛndʒərəs〕*adj.* 危險的
  ride〔raɪd〕*v.* 騎　without〔wɪðˈaʊt〕*prep.* 沒有
  helmet〔ˈhɛlmɪt〕*n.* 安全帽　protect〔prəˈtɛk〕*v.* 保護
  accident〔ˈæksədənt〕*n.* 意外

11. (**A**) Here is a book he likes very much. He has read it many times.

這裡有一本他非常喜歡的書。他已經讀了很多遍了。

空格原本須填入關係代名詞 which 或 that，引導形容詞子句，修飾先行詞 book，但如果關係代名詞在子句中做受詞時，則可以省略，故選 (A)。(B) who 修飾人，用法不合。

* time〔taɪm〕*n.* 次數

12. (**C**) John looks very old. In fact, he is only twenty years old.

約翰看起來年紀很大。事實上，他只有二十歲。

(A) by the way　順便一提
(B) so far　到目前為止
(C) *in fact*　事實上
(D) right away　馬上

13. (**D**) The <u>dialogue</u> in the cartoon "Pokemon" is quite funny.

「皮卡丘」這部卡通中的<u>對話</u>相當好笑。

    (A) cancer〔'kænsɚ〕 *n.* 癌症

    (B) factory〔'fæktrɪ〕 *n.* 工廠

    (C) answer〔'ænsɚ〕 *n.* 回答

    (D) *dialogue*〔'daɪə,lɔg〕 *n.* 對話

    * cartoon〔kɑr'tun〕 *n.* 卡通

    Pokemon〔'pokəmən〕 *n.* 皮卡丘 (日本卡通：口袋怪獸)

    quite〔kwaɪt〕 *adv.* 相當   funny〔'fʌnɪ〕 *adj.* 好笑的

14. (**B**) We will <u>celebrate</u> her fourteenth birthday by going out to a well-known restaurant.

我們到一家著名的餐廳用餐，<u>慶祝</u>她十四歲的生日。

    (A) review〔rɪ'vju〕 *v.* 複習

    (B) *celebrate*〔'sɛlə,bret〕 *v.* 慶祝

    (C) decorate〔'dɛkə,ret〕 *v.* 裝飾

    (D) surprise〔sə'praɪz〕 *v.* 使驚訝

    * *by* + *V-ing* 藉由~ (方法)   *go out* 外出

    well-known〔'wɛl'non〕 *adj.* 著名的

    restaurant〔'rɛstərənt〕 *n.* 餐廳

15. (**B**) Mary was given a lot of <u>presents</u> when she had her baby.

瑪麗生小孩時，收到許多<u>禮物</u>。

    (A) pond〔pɑnd〕 *n.* 池塘

    (B) *present*〔'prɛzn̩t〕 *n.* 禮物

    (C) parents〔'pɛrənts〕 *n. pl.* 父母

    (D) program〔'progræm〕 *n.* 節目

    * *have a baby* 生小孩

第二部份：段落填空

Questions 16-20

My junior high school days were really happy <u>ones</u> though a
₁₆

little boring sometimes. We had to take many tests every day,

and the thing <u>which</u> we had to do was study, study, and study.
₁₇

But it is <u>strange</u> that I loved those days. <u>Perhaps</u> it was because
₁₈ ₁₉

we only had to think about our studies. When I become a senior

high school student, I'll read many, many books <u>I like</u>. I know
₂₀

hard work will make me a great man one day.

　　我的國中生活，雖然有時候有點無聊，但大部份的時間都過得很快
樂。每天我們都有很多考試，除了唸書，還是唸書。不過奇怪的是，我
還蠻喜歡那段日子的。也許是因爲我們只需要考慮到唸書這件事吧。等
我成了高中生後，我要看很多我喜歡的書。我知道努力會使我將來有一
天，成爲一個大人物。

days〔dez〕*n. pl.*（特定的）時期　　though〔ðo〕*conj.* 雖然
a little 有一點（= *a little bit* = *a bit*）
boring〔'borɪŋ〕*adj.* 無聊的
sometimes〔'sʌm,taɪmz〕*adv.* 有時候　　***have to*** 必須
take〔tek〕*v.* 參加（考試）　　test〔tɛst〕*n.* 測驗；考試
think about 考慮　　studies〔'stʌdɪz〕*n. pl.* 學業
senior〔'sinjɚ〕*adj.* 高級的；年長的
senior high school 高中　　***hard work*** 努力
make〔mek〕*v.* 使成爲　　great〔gret〕*adj.* 偉大的
one day（將來）某天（= *some day*）

16. (**C**) *ones* 代替前面提到的複數可數名詞 days。

17. (**A**) 先行詞 the thing 是「事物」,關係代名詞須用 which 或 that,
引導形容詞子句,並在子句中,做動詞 do 的受詞。

18. (**D**) 依句意,選 (D) *strange*〔strendʒ〕*adj.* 奇怪的。而 (A) happy
「快樂的」,(B) fun「有趣的」,皆不合句意。(C) interest
〔'ɪntrɪst〕*n.* 興趣,為名詞,則用法不合。

19. (**C**) (A) When,(B) After,(D) If,均為連接詞,故用法不合,
選 (C) *Perhaps*〔pɚ'hæps〕*adv.* 或許。

20. (**D**) 空格應填入一形容詞子句,修飾先行詞 books,like 作「喜歡」
解時為及物動詞,不須接介系詞,故 (A) (B) 不合。(C) 須改為
(that) I'm interested in 或 that interest me,故選 (D) *I like*,
原本是 that I like,但關係代名詞 that 為形容詞子句中的受詞
時,可省略。

Questions 21-25

The Internet has changed the world a lot. At first, some parents did not like it because they thought it was <u>not good</u> for
21
their children. However, since they began to use the Net, they <u>have learned</u> that some sites are really helpful. The sites even
22
help children to study better. Although the sites <u>which</u> are most
23
interesting to children are <u>the ones</u> with lots of games, parents
24
are not worried anymore. They let their children play some games now. Today, <u>more and more</u> people find they cannot do
25
without the Net. It will surely become even more popular in the near future.

網際網路已經大幅度地改變這世界。起初,有些父母認爲網路對小孩不好,所以不喜歡網路。然而,自從他們開始使用網路,便知道有些網站真的很有幫助。而這些網站甚至幫助小孩書唸得更好。雖然對小孩子來說,最有趣的網站是有許多遊戲的網站,可是父母已經不再擔心了。現在他們也讓小孩玩些遊戲。現今有越來越多的人發現,他們不能沒有網路。在不久的將來,網路勢必會越來越普遍。

Internet〔'ɪntɚ,nɛt〕*n.* 網際網路 (= *Net*)
change〔tʃendʒ〕*v.* 改變　　***a lot*** 很多
at first 起初　　however〔hau'ɛvɚ〕*adv.* 然而
since〔sɪns〕*conj.* 自從　　begin〔bɪ'gɪn〕*v.* 開始
site〔saɪt〕*n.* 網站 (= *website*)

helpful〔'hɛlpfəl〕adj. 有幫助的
although〔ɔl'ðo〕conj. 雖然
interesting〔'ɪntrɪstɪŋ〕adj. 有趣的
lots of 很多的（= *a lot of*）
worried〔'wɝɪd〕adj. 擔心的
not…anymore 不再　　let〔lɛt〕v. 讓
cannot do without 不能沒有　　surely〔'ʃʊrlɪ〕adv. 必定地
even〔'ivən〕adv. 更加（加強比較級的語氣）
popular〔'pɑpjələ〕adj. 普遍的；受歡迎的
in the near future 在不久的將來

21.（**A**）依句意，有些父母不喜歡網路，是因他們認為網路對小孩而言，
　　　　　是「不好的」，故選 (A) ***not good***。

22.（**C**）since 引導的副詞子句中，動詞時態用過去式，而主要子句的
　　　　　動詞時態用「現在完成式」，表示「從過去繼續到現在的動作
　　　　　或狀態」，故選 (C) ***have learned***。

23.（**D**）先行詞 sites 為「事物」，故關係代名詞用 ***which***。

24.（**B**）one 可代替前面提到的名詞。本題中，***the ones*** = the sites。

25.（**D**）依句意，有「越來越多的」人覺得不能沒有網路，many 的比
　　　　　較級是 ***more***，故選 (D)。「比較級 + and + 比較級」是加強
　　　　　比較級語氣的用法。而 (A) fewer and fewer「越來越少」修
　　　　　飾可數名詞，(C) less and less「越來越少」修飾不可數名詞，
　　　　　均不合句意。

第三部份：閱讀理解

Questions 26-27

2002 年夏季舞會
國中生專屬派對

日期　：六月二十九日，星期六
　　　　七月二十八日，星期日
　　　　八月三十一日，星期六
地點　：台北青年學校
時間　：晚上六點至九點
費用　：每人新台幣三百元
電話　：(02) 2383-4949

攜伴參加，可以
得到一份神祕禮物！

---

dance〔dæns〕n. 舞會　　party〔'pɑrtɪ〕n. 派對
cost〔kɔst〕n. 費用　　Tel 電話 (*telephone* 的縮寫)
secret〔'sikrɪt〕*adj.* 秘密的　　present〔'prɛznt〕n. 禮物

26. (**C**) 派對 ＿＿＿＿＿＿＿。

　　(A) 進行的時間是兩個小時　　(B) 每個禮拜都有舉行
　　(C) 是在週末舉行的　　　　　(D) 是在春天和夏天舉行的
　　* hold〔hold〕v. 舉行　　weekend〔'wik'ɛnd〕n. 週末

27. (**D**) 何者為眞？

　　(A) 參加派對的人都可以得到一份禮物。
　　(B) 你應該獨自前往派對。
　　(C) 參加一次派對，須付四百元的費用。
　　(D) 今年夏天，台北青年學校將舉辦三場派對。

Questions 28-29

In the United States, it's usual to leave your waiter a tip—extra money for service. Before leaving the restaurant, you leave the tip on the table. Most people leave about 15% of the total bill. Look at Robert's check. Then answer the questions.

在美國，給服務生小費——也就是額外的服務費，是很平常的事。在離開餐廳之前，就把小費留在桌上。大部份的人，會留帳單全額的百分之十五的小費。請看羅伯特的帳單，然後回答問題。

漢堡	2.15
炸雞	4.15
稅	0.70
合計	7.00

usual〔'juʒʊəl〕adj. 常見的（= common）
leave〔liv〕v. 留…給（人）；離開　　waiter〔'wetɚ〕n. 服務生
tip〔tɪp〕n. 小費　　extra〔'ɛkstrə〕adj. 額外的
service〔'sɝvɪs〕n. 服務　　total〔'totḷ〕adj. n. 總額（的）
bill〔bɪl〕n. 帳單（= check〔tʃɛk〕）
hamburger〔'hæmbɝgɚ〕n. 漢堡　　fried〔fraɪd〕adj. 油炸的
chicken〔'tʃɪkən〕n. 雞肉　　tax〔tæks〕n. 稅

28. (**C**)　羅伯特必須付美金 ＿＿＿＿＿＿＿ 元。
　　　(A) 6.30　　　(B) 7.90　　　(C) 7.00　　　(D) 6.75

29. (**C**)　羅伯特可能會留美金 ＿＿＿＿＿＿＿ 元的小費。
　　　(A) 0.33　　　(B) 0.69　　　(C) 1.05　　　(D) 1.50
　　　* probably〔'prabəblɪ〕adv. 可能　　7.00×15% = 1.05（元）

<u>Questions 30-31</u>

Have you ever wanted to write a song? Two sisters, Mildred and Patty Hill, once <u>composed</u> a little song. It was a happy song that they loved to sing. It was called "Good Morning to You." However, most other people didn't know the song very well.

你曾想過要寫歌嗎？一對叫做米爾德・希爾和派蒂・希爾的姊妹，就曾經作了一首簡短的歌曲。那是一首她們喜歡哼唱的快樂歌曲，叫做「向你道聲早安」。然而，大部份的人都不太知道這首歌。

once〔wʌns〕adv. 曾經　　compose〔kəmˈpoz〕v. 作曲
call〔kɔl〕v. 稱為　　however〔hauˈɛvɚ〕adv. 然而

One day, Mildred and Patty had an idea. It turned out to be a very good idea. They decided to change the words of the song. They called the new song "Happy Birthday to You."

有一天，米爾德和派蒂想到一個點子。這點子結果變成一個非常好的點子。她們決定把歌詞改掉。她們把這首新歌命名為「祝你生日快樂」。

one day　（過去）某日　　**turn out**　結果
idea〔aɪˈdiə〕n. 主意；點子　　decide〔dɪˈsaɪd〕v. 決定
words〔wɝdz〕n. pl. 歌詞

Their short birthday song is now very famous. Almost everyone knows the words. Did anyone sing it at your last birthday?

這首簡短的歌曲現在非常有名。幾乎每個人都知道歌詞。上次你過生日時，有人唱這首歌嗎？

famous〔ˈfeməs〕adj. 有名的　　almost〔ˈɔl.most〕adv. 幾乎
last〔læst〕adj. 上一次的

30. (**A**) 最適合的標題是 ＿＿＿＿＿＿＿＿。

(A) 一首著名歌曲的由來　　(B) 向你道聲早安

(C) 為什麼人們愛唱歌　　　(D) 每個人都有生日

* title〔ˋtaɪtḷ〕 n. 標題

31. (**C**) 第二行裡的 "composed" 意思是 ＿＿＿＿＿＿＿＿。

(A) 遺失　　　　　　　　(B) 告訴

(C) 寫　　　　　　　　　(D) 忘記

* line〔laɪn〕 n. 行　　 mean〔min〕 v. 意思是
lose〔luz〕 v. 遺失　　forget〔fɚˋgɛt〕 v. 忘記

Questions 32-33

The hummingbird is an amazing animal! It can actually
flap its wings back and forth seventy-five times a second!
This fast movement helps the hummingbird stay in midair
while feeding from flowers. Its wings move so fast that they
look like a blur.

蜂鳥是一種驚人的動物！事實上，牠們能夠每秒鐘來回拍動翅膀七
十五下！如此快速的振動使蜂鳥從花朵覓食時，能停留在半空中。蜂鳥
拍動翅膀的速度很快，因此看起來就像是模模糊糊的一點。

hummingbird〔ˋhʌmɪŋ͵bɝd〕 n. 蜂鳥
amazing〔əˋmezɪŋ〕 adj. 驚人的　　animal〔ˋænəml〕 n. 動物
actually〔ˋæktʃʊəlɪ〕 adv. 事實上　　flap〔flæp〕 v. 拍動
wing〔wɪŋ〕 n. 翅膀　　 **back and forth** 來回地
second〔ˋsɛkənd〕 n. 秒　　movement〔ˋmuvmənt〕 n. 動作
stay〔ste〕 v. 停留　　midair〔͵mɪdˋɛr〕 n. 空中
feed〔fid〕 v. 吃東西　　 **so⋯that~** 如此⋯以致於~
blur〔blɝ〕 n. 模糊而看不清楚的東西

Not only is the hummingbird fast, but it is also very small, often measuring only two or four inches in length. Hummingbird babies are usually not much bigger than bumblebees.

蜂鳥不僅動作快,體型也很小,通常只有二到四英吋長。幼鳥通常沒比土蜂大多少。

> ***not only…but also~*** 不但…而且~
> measure〔ˈmɛʒɚ〕v. 有…(長、寬、高)
> inch〔ɪntʃ〕n. 英吋(1 英吋等於 2.54 公分)
> length〔lɛŋθ〕n. 長度
> bumblebee〔ˈbʌmbḷ͵bi〕n. 大黃蜂;土蜂

Although hummingbirds are very small, they are not weak. They have <u>adapted</u> to many different kinds of climates. These little birds can be found all over the Americas—from the southern tip of South America to the lands of the Arctic.

蜂鳥體型雖小,可是體力一點也不差。牠們能夠適應多種不同的氣候。這些小鳥的活動範圍遍及整個美洲大陸——從南美州的最南端,一直到北極圈之內的土地。

> although〔ɔlˈðo〕conj. 雖然   weak〔wik〕adj. 虛弱的
> adapt〔əˈdæpt〕v. 適應 < to >   different〔ˈdɪfrənt〕adj. 不同的
> kind〔kaɪnd〕n. 種類   climate〔ˈklaɪmɪt〕n. 氣候
> ***all over*** 遍及   Americas〔əˈmɛrɪkəz〕n. pl. 美洲大陸
> southern〔ˈsʌðɚn〕adj. 南方的   tip〔tɪp〕n. 尖端
> ***South America*** 南美洲   land〔lænd〕n. 土地
> Arctic〔ˈɑrktɪk〕n. 北極

32. (**B**) 最適合的標題是 ＿＿＿＿＿＿＿＿ 。

    (A) 居住於各地的鳥類   (B) <u>驚人的蜂鳥</u>

    (C) 蜂鳥的翅膀   (D) 體型極小的鳥

33. (**B**) 第十行裡的 "adapted" 意思是 ＿＿＿＿＿＿ 。

(A) 下蛋　　　　　　　　　　(B) 為了適應而改變

(C) 無法改變　　　　　　　　(D) 改變顏色

＊ lay〔le〕v. 下蛋（三態變化為：lay-laid-laid）

egg〔εg〕n. 蛋　　fit〔fɪt〕v. 適應

fail to + V. 未能　　color〔'kʌlɚ〕n. 顏色

Questions 34-35

The street lamps are shaped like chocolate candy "Kisses."
The streets have names like East Chocolate Avenue. You are in
Chocolate Town, U.S.A. Its real name is Hershey, Pennsylvania.

街燈的形狀就和 Kisses 巧克力糖一樣。街道則取像東巧克力大街這
樣的名字。你現在置身於美國的巧克力城。這城市的真正名稱是賓州的
赫喜城。

lamp〔læmp〕n. 燈　　　***street lamp*** 街燈

shape〔ʃep〕v. 把…造成（某種形狀）

be shaped like 形狀就像

chocolate〔'tʃɔklɪt〕n. 巧克力　　avenue〔'ævə,nju〕n. 大街

town〔taʊn〕n. 城鎮　　real〔'riəl〕adj. 真正的

Pennsylvania〔,pεnsḷ'venjə〕n. 賓夕法尼亞州（位於美東，略稱賓州）

In 1905, a man named Milton Hershey opened a chocolate
factory in a cornfield. Today there are thousands of people
living in the town. Visitors are amazed at the huge <u>vats</u> that hold
ten thousand pounds of chocolate each. It takes milk from fifty
thousand cows every day to help make the candy. There are
barns holding 90 million pounds of cacao beans. Chocolate is
made from cacao beans.

在西元一九〇五年，一位名叫米爾頓·赫喜的人，在玉米田開了一間巧克力工廠。現今有數千位鎮民居住於此。觀光客對那些可容納一萬磅巧克力的<u>大桶子</u>感到驚奇。每天需要五萬頭母牛的牛奶，來生產巧克力。這裡的穀倉，可容納九千萬磅的可可豆。巧克力就是由可可豆製成的。

name〔nem〕v. 給…取名　　factory〔'fæktrɪ〕n. 工廠
cornfield〔'kɔrn‚fild〕n. 玉米田
thousands of 數以千計的　　visitor〔'vɪzɪtɚ〕n. 遊客
amazed〔ə'mezd〕adj. 感到驚訝的 < at >
huge〔hjudʒ〕adj. 巨大的　　vat〔væt〕n. 大桶
hold〔hold〕v. 容納；裝　　***ten thousand*** 一萬
pound〔paʊnd〕n. 磅（重量單位）　　cow〔kaʊ〕n. 母牛
barn〔bɑrn〕n. 穀倉　　million〔'mɪljən〕n. 百萬
cacao〔kə'keo〕n. 可可　　bean〔bin〕n. 豆
be made from 由…所製成

If you are ever near Hershey, Pennsylvania, stop at the world's largest chocolate factory. There are free samples, too!

如果你有機會到賓州的赫喜城附近，要到全世界最大的巧克力工廠停留一下。那裡也有免費的試吃品！

stop〔stɑp〕v. 停留　　free〔fri〕adj. 免費的
sample〔'sæmpḷ〕n. 試用品

34. (**D**) 第七行裡的 "vats" 意思是 ＿＿＿＿＿＿。

(A) 人們　　(B) 豆子　　(C) 杯子　　(D) <u>箱子</u>

* tank〔tæŋk〕n. 箱；槽

35. (**C**) 從工廠的規模來看，你可以判斷出人們喜歡 ＿＿＿＿＿＿。

(A) 牛奶　　(B) 可可豆　　(C) <u>巧克力</u>　　(D) 觀光客

* size〔saɪz〕n. 尺寸；大小　　tell〔tɛl〕v. 知道

三、寫作能力測驗

第一部份：單句寫作

第 1~5 題：句子改寫

1. Swimming in the river is dangerous.

   It's _____.

   　重點結構：以 It 為虛主詞引導的句子

   　　解　答：It's dangerous to swim in the river.

   　句型分析：It's + 形容詞 + to V.

   　　說　明：虛主詞 it 代替不定詞片語，不定詞片語則擺在句
   　　　　　　尾，故 swimming in the river 改為 to swim in
   　　　　　　the river。

   　* swim〔swɪm〕v. 游泳　　river〔'rɪvɚ〕n. 河
   　　dangerous〔'dendʒərəs〕adj. 危險的

2. I got someone to mail the letter yesterday.

   I had _____.

   　重點結構：「have + sb. + 原形動詞」的用法

   　　解　答：I had someone mail the letter yesterday.

   　句型分析：主詞 + have + 受詞 + 原形動詞

   　　說　明：「get + sb. + to V.」表「叫某人做～」，若用
   　　　　　　使役動詞 have，接受詞後，須用原形動詞。

   　* mail〔mel〕v. 郵寄　　letter〔'lɛtɚ〕n. 信

3. You enjoy roller-skating, and he does, too.
   Not only _____.

　　重點結構：「not only…but also~」的用法
　　　解　答：<u>Not only you but also he enjoys roller-skating.</u>
　　句型分析：Not only + A + but also + B + 動詞
　　　説　明：「not only A but also B」表「不但 A，而且 B」，
　　　　　　　做主詞時，動詞的單複數視 B 來決定，因為此片語
　　　　　　　的強調部份是 B。這裡的 he 是第三人稱單數，故動
　　　　　　　詞用 enjoys。
　　* roller-skate〔'rolə‚sket〕v. 輪式溜冰

4. Every time she comes, she must bring a present to us.
   She never comes _____.

　　重點結構：「never + 一般動詞 + without + 動名詞」的用法
　　　解　答：<u>She never comes without bringing a present to us.</u>
　　句型分析：主詞 + never + 動詞 + without + 動名詞
　　　説　明：按照句意，「每當她來訪時，她一定帶禮物給我們。」
　　　　　　　這題若用 never（絕不）表示否定的句意，又接
　　　　　　　without（沒有），為雙重否定，表「每…必~」。
　　　　　　　without 為介系詞，後面須接動名詞。
　　* *every time* 每當

5. Where is the nearest police station?
   Tell me _____.

　　重點結構：間接問句做名詞子句
　　　解　答：<u>Tell me where the nearest police station is.</u>

句型分析：Tell me + where + 主詞 + 動詞

　説　明：在 wh-問句前加 Tell me，形成間接問句，必須把 be 動詞 is 放在最後面，並把問號改成句點。

* ***police station*** 警察局

第 6～10 題：句子合併

6. My father painted the house.

I helped my father.

　　　　　　　　　　　　　　　　　　　　　.

重點結構：「help + *sb.* + (to) V.」的用法

　解　答：I helped my father (to) paint the house.

句型分析：help + 受詞 + 原形動詞或不定詞

　説　明：句意是「我幫爸爸油漆房子」，用動詞 help 造句，help 之後所接的不定詞的 to 可省略。

* paint〔pent〕*v.* 油漆

7. I'm talking about that stranger.

That stranger is wearing a red sweater.（用 in 合併）

　　　　　　　　　　　　　　　　　　　　　.

重點結構：in 的用法

　解　答：I'm talking about that stranger in a red sweater.

句型分析：名詞 + in + 衣服

　説　明：wearing a red sweater 可改成 in a red sweater，修飾 that stranger。

* ***talk about*** 談論　　stranger〔'strendʒɚ〕*n.* 陌生人

sweater〔'swɛtɚ〕*n.* 毛衣

8. Mr. Lin invited the woman.

The woman is not very tall. (用 who 合併)

_____.

重點結構：由 who 引導的形容詞子句

解　答：<u>Mr. Lin invited the woman who is not very tall.</u>

句型分析：Mr. Lin invited the woman ＋ who ＋ 動詞

說　明：句意是「林先生邀請那位長得不是很高的女士」，在合併兩句時，用 who 代替先行詞 the woman，引導形容詞子句，在子句中做主詞。

* invite〔ɪn'vaɪt〕v. 邀請

9. Linda looks very funny.

Linda wears that cowboy hat. (用 if 合併)

_____.

重點結構：由連接詞 if 引導的副詞子句

解　答：<u>Linda looks very funny if she wears that cowboy hat.</u>

句型分析：Linda looks very funny ＋ if ＋ 主詞 ＋ 動詞

說　明：按照句意，「琳達如果戴上那頂牛仔帽，會看起來很好笑」。用連接詞 if 連接兩句時，if 要引導完整的子句，即「if ＋ 主詞 ＋ 動詞」。

* funny〔'fʌnɪ〕adj. 好笑的
  cowboy hat 牛仔帽

10. Miss White moved the heavy box.

No one helped her with it. (用反身代名詞合併)

_____.

重點結構：「by + 反身代名詞」的用法

解　答：Miss White moved the heavy box by herself.

句型分析：主詞 + 動詞 + 受詞 + by + 反身代名詞

說　明：由 No one helped her with it. 可知「懷特小姐自己
　　　　一個人搬運很重的箱子」，用片語「by *oneself*」，
　　　　表「獨力；靠自己」，Miss White 為女性第三人稱
　　　　單數，故反身代名詞用 herself。

* move〔muv〕*v.* 移動；搬動

第 11～15 題：重組

11. Ronald's _____.

been / away / several times / has / car / towed

重點結構：現在完成式字序及被動語態字序

解　答：Ronald's car has been towed away several times.

句型分析：主詞 + have/has + been + 過去分詞

說　明：一般現在完成式的結構是「主詞 + have/has + 過去
　　　　分詞」，而一般被動語態的結構是「主詞 + be 動詞
　　　　+ 過去分詞」，be 動詞的現在完成式是 have/has
　　　　been，故形成此句。

* *tow away* 拖吊　　several〔'sɛvərəl〕*adj.* 好幾個

12. It's _____.

　　others / wrong / copy / your answers / to let

　　　　重點結構：以 It 為虛主詞引導的句子

　　　　　解　答：It's wrong to let others copy your answers.

　　　　句型分析：It's ＋ 形容詞 ＋ to V.

　　　　　說　明：先找出形容詞 wrong 之後，找出不定詞 to let，
　　　　　　　　　　又 let 為使役動詞，接受詞後，須接原形動詞。

　　　　＊ wrong〔rɔŋ〕adj. 不對的　　copy〔ˈkɑpɪ〕v. 抄寫

13. Judy _____.

　　to / be / too / is / on the school / short / basketball team

　　　　重點結構：「too ＋ 形容詞 ＋ to V.」的用法

　　　　　解　答：Judy is too short to be on the school basketball
　　　　　　　　　　team.

　　　　句型分析：主詞 ＋ be 動詞 ＋ too ＋ 形容詞 ＋ to V.

　　　　　說　明：這題的意思是說「茱蒂長得太矮，不能參加籃球
　　　　　　　　　　校隊」，用「too…to V.」合併兩句，表「太…
　　　　　　　　　　而不能～」。

　　　　＊ team〔tim〕n. 隊

14. The question _____.

　　children / answer it / that / is / hard / can't / so

　　　　重點結構：「so ＋ 形容詞 ＋ that 子句」的用法

　　　　　解　答：The question is so hard that children can't
　　　　　　　　　　answer it.

句型分析：主詞＋be 動詞＋so＋形容詞＋that＋主詞＋動詞

說　明：這題的意思是說「這問題太難了，所以小孩答不出來」，合併兩句時，用「so…that～」，表「如此…以致於～」。

* hard〔hɑrd〕*adj.* 困難的

15. People _____.
water / might / their health / afraid / that / are / harm / pollution

重點結構：「be 動詞＋afraid＋that＋主詞＋動詞」的用法

解　答：<u>People are afraid that water pollution might harm their health.</u>

句型分析：主詞＋be 動詞＋afraid＋that＋主詞＋動詞

說　明：afraid（害怕的）的用法為：

$$\begin{cases} \text{be 動詞＋afraid of＋N / V-ing} \\ \text{be 動詞＋afraid＋that＋主詞＋動詞} \end{cases}$$

* pollution〔pə'luʃən〕*n.* 污染
  harm〔hɑrm〕*v.* 傷害　　health〔hɛlθ〕*n.* 健康

第二部份：段落寫作

題目：這是妳／你一天的生活，請根據圖片內容寫一篇約 50 字的簡短
　　　描述。

I usually get up *at six o'clock*. I start my day by brushing my teeth and washing my face. ***Then*** I have my breakfast before going to school. I arrive at school at seven thirty. At school, I have a lot of classes, like math, science, and music. I come home *at four o'clock*. After dinner, I do my homework. ***When it's nine o'clock***, I go to bed and hope that I have a sweet dream.

get up 起床　　teeth 〔 tiθ 〕 *n. pl.* 牙齒
brush 〔 brʌʃ 〕 *v.* 刷　　face 〔 fes 〕 *n.* 臉
have 〔 hæv 〕 *v.* 吃　　arrive 〔 əˈraɪv 〕 *v.* 到達
science 〔ˈsaɪəns 〕 *n.* 自然科學　　hope 〔 hop 〕 *v.* 希望
sweet 〔 swit 〕 *adj.* 甜美的　　dream 〔 drim 〕 *n.* 夢

全民英語能力分級檢定測驗

初級測驗②

本測驗分三部份，全為三選一之選擇題，每部份各 10 題，共 30 題，作答時間約 20 分鐘。

第一部份： 看圖辨義

本部份共 10 題，試題冊上每題有一個圖片，請聽錄音機播出一個相關的問題，與 A、B、C 三個英語敘述後，選一個與所看到圖片最相符的答案，並在答案紙上相對的圓圈內塗黑作答。每題播出一遍，問題及選項均不印在試題冊上。

例：（看）

NT$80   NT$50

（聽）

Look at the picture. How much is the hamburger?

  A. It's eighty dollars.

  B. It's fifty-five dollars.

  C. It's eighteen dollars.

正確答案為 A

Question 1

Question 2

Question 3

Question 4

Question 5

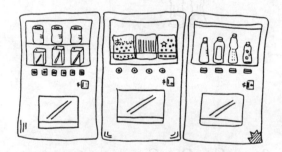

Question 6

請 翻 頁 ⫸

Question 7

Question 8

Question 9

Question 10

請翻頁

第二部份： 問答

本部份共 10 題，每題錄音機會播出一個問句或直述句，
每題播出一次，聽後請從試題冊上 A、B、C 三個選項
中，選出一個最適合的回答或回應，並在答案紙上塗黑
作答。

例：

（聽） Good morning, Kevin. How are you?

（看） A. I'm fine, thank you.
B. I'm in the living room.
C. My name is Kevin.

正確答案為 A

11. A. Yes, we're having
great weather.
B. Thank you.
C. It was a gift from my
mother.

12. A. I don't, cither.
B. No problem.
C. I'll get it.

13. A. He is fine, thank you.
B. They are all fine,
thank you.
C. It's the best.

14. A. I could tell time when
I was five years old.
B. I will have some free
time after lunch.
C. Sorry, I don't have
a watch either.

15. A. Time to go to class.
    B. It's for you.
    C. Who's at the door?

16. A. My math book is blue.
    B. I'm not good at
       math either.
    C. It's on the desk.

17. A. We go home at 4:30.
    B. I can get out of class
       when I am sick.
    C. I didn't get a lot out
       of that class.

18. A. Mine, too.
    B. I also love food.
    C. I'll have a medium.

19. A. I'd like some beef
       noodles.
    B. I'd never desert you.
    C. Nothing for me,
       thanks.

20. A. She is very tall and
       thin.
    B. She is sixteen.
    C. She is fine.

請 翻 頁 ◀️━━▷

第三部份：　簡短對話

　　　　　本部份共 10 題，每題錄音機會播出一段對話及一個相關
　　　　　的問題，每題播出兩次，聽後請從試題冊上 A、B、C 三
　　　　　個選項中，選出一個最適合的回答，並在答案紙上塗黑
　　　　　作答。

　　　例：

　　　（聽）(Woman)　Good afternoon, ...Mr. Davis?

　　　　　(Man)　　　Yes.　I have an appointment with
　　　　　　　　　　Dr. Sanders at two o'clock.　My
　　　　　　　　　　son Tommy has a fever.

　　　　　(Woman)　Oh, that's too bad.　Well, please
　　　　　　　　　　have a seat, Mr. Davis.　Dr.
　　　　　　　　　　Sanders will be right with you.

　　　　　Question:　Where did this conversation take
　　　　　　　　　　place?

　　　（看）A.　In a post office.

　　　　　B.　In a restaurant.

　　　　　C.　In a doctor's office.

　　　　　正確答案爲 C

21. A. She will change trains
       at Mill Town at 6:00.
    B. She will take the 6:00
       train to West Branch.
    C. She will take a bus
       from Mill Town.

22. A. The plane is about to
       take off.
    B. There is no drinking
       allowed on the flight.
    C. He does not have
       enough money to
       pay for it.

23. A. He is going to the
       movies.
    B. It's not his turn to do
       housework.
    C. He has too much
       homework to do.

24. A. He was late for school.
    B. He was exercising.
    C. He is out of shape.

25. A. She wants the man to
       help her carry the
       books.
    B. She wants to give
       the man some books.
    C. She wants to open a
       bookstore.

26. A. He doesn't know
       where Central
       Avenue is.
    B. He doesn't know
       how to draw a map.
    C. He doesn't know
       where the woman's
       house is.

27. A. The woman will drive
       her parents' new car.
    B. The man's parents
       will drive them.
    C. The woman's brother
       will take them.

請 翻 頁 ⊫⟹

28. A. He should take a rest.
    B. He should take some medicine.
    C. He should see a doctor tomorrow.

29. A. John and Alice got married.
    B. John told the woman he will marry Alice.
    C. John asked Alice to marry him.

30. A. He thinks the woman should get to know his parents better.
    B. He thinks the woman should study computer science.
    C. He thinks the woman should major in biology.

二、閱讀能力測驗

本測驗分三部份，全為四選一之選擇題，共 35 題，作答時間 35 分鐘。

第一部份： 詞彙和結構

本部份共15題，每題含一個空格。請就試題冊上 A、B、C、D 四個選項中選出最適合題意的字或詞，標示在答案紙上。

1. It took Peter a long time to find a job after he left school. _____ last, he found a job as a teacher.
   A. In
   B. At
   C. On
   D. To

2. Mr. Brown _____ to America, so he isn't here now.
   A. has come
   B. is going
   C. has gone
   D. has been

3. It's _____ for people under 20 to drive a car in Taiwan.
   A. humid
   B. active
   C. comfortable
   D. illegal

請 翻 頁 ⬅️➡️

4. _____ Christmas Eve, we'll have a big dinner and then we'll go to church together.

    A. At

    B. In

    C. For

    D. On

5. Not only you but also I _____ right, so we don't have to fight about this.

    A. am

    B. are

    C. is

    D. have

6. I have three brothers. One is a teacher, and _____ are businessmen.

    A. another

    B. the others

    C. the other

    D. others

7. There is a "No Parking" sign over there. Your car will _____ away if you park your car there.

    A. be towed

    B. towed

    C. have towed

    D. tow

8. Christmas is coming, and everything in the department store is _____ sale.
   A. having
   B. in
   C. on
   D. at

9. The shirts need _____, but you don't have to do it now.
   A. to wash
   B. washed
   C. washing
   D. to be wash

10. Could you please stop _____ so much noise? We are in a hospital, and the patients need some rest.
    A. to make
    B. making
    C. to be made
    D. has made

11. There is a shortage of water because there has been very _____ rain recently.
    A. few
    B. a few
    C. little
    D. a little

請 翻 頁 ◀▭⟹

12. I borrowed your pen without asking first, and I lost it. I
    don't know _____ to do.
    A. what
    B. how
    C. which
    D. who

13. When he took off his hat, I _____ that he was bald.
    A. produced
    B. imagined
    C. noticed
    D. surprised

14. Matt : _____ do you go to cram school?
    Leo : Four times a week.
    A. How many
    B. How often
    C. How long
    D. How old

15. She looks only 30, but in fact she's much _____ than
    she looks.
    A. old
    B. older
    C. oldest
    D. the oldest

第二部份： 段落填空

　　　　本部份共 10 題，包括二個段落，每個段落各含 5 個空格。
　　　　請就試題冊上 A、B、C、D 四個選項中選出最適合題意
　　　　的字或詞，標示在答案紙上。

Questions 16-20

　　Tina went to Taipei Zoo ____(16)____ January 25. It was her
birthday. She got up early that day, and then she ____(17)____
her friends at the MRT station. They spent twenty minutes
____(18)____ the MRT. ____(19)____ they got there, it started to rain.
But they didn't want to give ____(20)____. After a while, the rain
stopped. They had a very good time on that day.

16. A. in
　　B. at
　　C. on
　　D. for

19. A. Although
　　B. Because
　　C. When
　　D. If

17. A. meet
　　B. meets
　　C. meeting
　　D. met

20. A. up
　　B. down
　　C. for
　　D. with

18. A. take
　　B. taking
　　C. to take
　　D. took

請翻頁 ▷

Questions 21-25

Chinese New Year is a special holiday for everyone. At that time, family members ___(21)___ all over Taiwan get together. They ___(22)___ talking, eating, and having a good time.

Older family members talk about work and friends. They share news of the last year. Younger people have fun ___(23)___. They also get red envelopes with "lucky money" inside.

It's also a time to welcome the new year. People clean their houses. Friends visit each other. And people ___(24)___ each other good luck.

There's probably only one ___(25)___ thing about Chinese New Year: traffic. People say that on some days, the road from Keelung to Kaohsiung is like the world's biggest parking lot!

21. A. of
    B. in
    C. for
    D. from

22. A. enjoy
    B. plan
    C. want
    D. hate

23. A. play
    B. to play
    C. playing
    D. to playing

24. A. hope
    B. wish
    C. speak
    D. say

25. A. good
    B. kind
    C. nice
    D. terrible

第三部份：閱讀理解

　　本部份共 10 題，包括數段短文，每段短文後有 1～3 個相關問題，請就試題冊上 A、B、C、D 四個選項中選出最適合者，標示在答案紙上。

Question 26

WANTED

➢ a male under 30
➢ good command of English
➢ one year of teaching experience

☎ 2876-5432　　MR. WHITE

26. What kind of person does Mr. White want?

A. A teacher.

B. A secretary.

C. A singer.

D. A cook.

請 翻 頁 ▷

Questions 27-28

A	B	註：
32 years old 3 bdrm, 2 ba 2 lvrm, 1 ktch $180,000 2000 sq. ft	10 years old 3 bdrm, 1 ba 2 lvrm, 1 ktch $170,000 1450 sq. ft	bdrm（臥室） ba（浴室） lvrm（客廳） ktch（廚房） sq. ft（平方英呎）
C	D	
12 years old 2 bdrm, 1 ba 1 lvrm, 1 ktch $165,000 1654 sq. ft	25 years old 4 bdrm, 2 ba 2 lvrm, 2 ktch $280,000 3100 sq. ft	

27. Which house was built in 1990?

28. Mr. and Mrs. White have three little children. They are buying a house for all the family. They want to give each child a bedroom. Which house is the best for them?

Questions 29-30

A Birthday Party

Scottie White is invited to Grace Brown's 14th birthday party on Saturday, January 1st. The party will start at 6:00 p.m. and conclude at 9:30 p.m. It will be held at 252, Tien-mu W. Rd. Please call me at 2871-8125. See you Saturday.

29. How long will the party be?

    A. Two hours.

    B. Three hours.

    C. We don't know.

    D. Less than four hours.

30. Where will the party be?

    A. In the living room.

    B. We don't know.

    C. In the factory.

    D. In the kitchen.

請 翻 頁 ◀▯▯⟹

Questions 31-33

Many people think the English do not like to speak other languages. In fact, English is a mixture of words from many different languages. Because of this, the vocabulary of the English language is very large. It is much larger than that of almost every other language in the world.

Many English words come from Latin, the old language of Rome, and also from ancient Greek. From Latin we get words like "wine," "use" and "day." From Greek we have words such as "photograph," "Bible" and "ink." Because these two languages are dead, the words have most often come through other languages such as French, or the old German languages. There are also many words from both Greek and Latin together—"television," for example. Here "tele" is Greek for "far" and "vision" comes from Latin and means "seeing."

31. In ancient times, what language did the Romans speak?
    A. English.
    B. French.
    C. Latin.
    D. Greek.

32. Why is the English vocabulary very large?

   A. Because English itself has borrowed a lot of words from many different languages.

   B. Because English is the language with the longest history.

   C. Because English is used by most people.

   D. Because English is a living language.

33. What languages does the English word "television" come from?

   A. Latin.

   B. Greek.

   C. Latin and Greek.

   D. German.

請 翻 頁 ◀▭▭⟹

Questions 34-35

　　I was busy looking for two free tickets to a rock concert when my little sister Lisa came into my room. She wanted to tell me something but I was not interested. I pushed her out and closed the door behind her. Twenty minutes later, I gave up and called Jimmy. "Jimmy, I'm sorry that we can't go to the concert tonight. I've lost the tickets." Jimmy angrily hung up the phone and I felt very upset. Later that evening, Lisa handed me the concert tickets I had lost. "I wanted to give them to you, but you were so angry. I found them at your door, so I think they're yours, right? Are you still angry now?" she asked. "It's too late. But never mind. Thank you, anyway," I answered weakly.

34. Where did Lisa find the two tickets?
　　A. In the living room.
　　B. In the kitchen.
　　C. At the door of the bathroom.
　　D. At the door of the writer's room.

35. Which one is true?
　　A. Jimmy was happy to know what happened.
　　B. The writer and Jimmy went to the concert at last.
　　C. Lisa found the tickets and gave them to the writer.
　　D. Jimmy found the tickets.

三、寫作能力測驗

本測驗共有兩部份，第一部份為單句寫作，第二部份為段落寫作。測驗時間為 40 分鐘。

第一部份： 單句寫作
請將答案寫在寫作能力測驗答案紙對應的題號旁，如有拼字、標點、大小寫之錯誤，將予扣分。

第 1~5 題： 句子改寫
請依題目之提示，將原句改寫成指定型式，並將改寫的句子完整地寫在答案紙上（包括提示之文字及標點符號）。

1. Bob ： Did you remember to feed the dog?

   Sarah ： Yes, I did.

   Sarah remembered ＿＿＿＿＿＿＿＿＿＿.

2. Watching American movies on TV helps me learn English.

   It ＿＿＿＿＿＿＿＿＿＿＿＿＿＿＿＿.

3. Amy played basketball with her friends.

   When ＿＿＿＿＿＿＿＿＿＿＿＿＿＿?

4. How does Joseph go to school?

   I don't know ＿＿＿＿＿＿＿＿＿＿＿.

5. Jason cleaned the classroom. （用被動式）

   The classroom ＿＿＿＿＿＿＿＿＿＿＿.

請翻頁 ▐▌⟹

第6～10題：句子合併

請依照題目指示，將兩句合併成一句，並將合併的句子完整地寫在答案紙上（包括提示之文字及標點符號）。

6. Megan asked Carrie something. (用 why)
   Mark was late for school today.

   _____?

7. We visited Boston.
   We visited New York. (用 both…and～)

   _____

8. The TV program is exciting.
   Danny watches the TV program again. (用 enough)

   _____.

9. Here is a magazine.
   I enjoy the magazine very much. (用 which)

   _____.

10. The farmer sold fruit.
    The farmer made a lot of money. (用 by)

    _____.

請翻頁 ▷

第 11～15 題：重組

請將題目中所有提示字詞整合成一有意義的句子，並將重組的句子完整地寫在答案紙上（包括提示之文字及標點符號）。答案中必須使用所有提示字詞，且不能隨意增加字詞，否則不予計分。

11. Children _____.
   presents / mothers / on / their / buy / Mother's Day

12. Here _____.
   the / comes / bus

13. Tina _____.
   studied / two / for / English / has / years

14. Peter asked Jean _____.
   she / a / boyfriend / had / whether

15. Jimmy _____.
   such / everyone / a / boy / him / handsome / loves / is / that

請 翻 頁 ▷

第二部份：段落寫作

題目：今天是除夕夜，你／妳許下新年新希望，請根據圖片內容寫
　　　一篇約 50 字的簡短描述。

初級英檢模擬試題詳解②

一、聽力測驗

第一部份

Look at the picture for question 1.

1. (**B**) What are they doing?

A. They are riding a tricycle.

B. They are riding a motorbike.

C. They are riding a tandem bike.

* tricycle (ˈtraɪsɪkl̩) *n.* 三輪車
motorbike (ˈmotəˌbaɪk) *n.* 機車 (= *motorcycle*)
tandem (ˈtændəm) *n.* 協力車

Look at the picture for question 2.

2. (**B**) What is the policeman doing?

A. He is talking to the man.

B. He is giving the man a ticket.

C. He is giving the man directions.

* policeman (pəˈlismən) *n.* 警察　　ticket (ˈtɪkɪt) *n.* 罰單
direction (dəˈrɛkʃən) *n.* 方向

Look at the picture for question 3.

3. (**A**) What is the woman doing?

A. She is teaching.

B. She is studying.

C. She is writing.

Look at the picture for question 4.

4. (**C**)　What is the lady having for dinner?

　　　　A.　She is having rice.

　　　　B.　She is having beef.

　　　　C.　She is having chicken.

　　　* lady〔'ledɪ〕*n.* 女士　　rice〔raɪs〕*n.* 米飯
　　　　beef〔bif〕*n.* 牛肉　　chicken〔'tʃɪkən〕*n.* 雞肉

Look at the picture for question 5.

5. (**B**)　What are these?

　　　　A.　These are trash cans.

　　　　B.　These are vending machines.

　　　　C.　These are phone booths.

　　　* ***trash can*** 垃圾筒
　　　　vending machine 自動販賣機
　　　　phone booth 電話亭

Look at the picture for question 6.

6. (**C**)　Where is he?

　　　　A.　He is at the lawyer's office.

　　　　B.　He is at the post office.

　　　　C.　He is at the dentist's office.

　　　* lawyer〔'lɔjɚ〕*n.* 律師
　　　　office〔'ɔfɪs〕*n.* 辦公室；診療室
　　　　post office 郵局
　　　　dentist〔'dɛntɪst〕*n.* 牙醫

Look at the picture for question 7.

7. (**B**)　What does Jennifer like to do?

　　A.　She likes to play the guitar.

　　B.　She likes to play the violin.

　　C.　She likes to play the cello.

　　* guitar〔gɪˈtɑr〕*n.* 吉他

　　　violin〔͵vaɪəˈlɪn〕*n.* 小提琴

　　　cello〔ˈtʃɛlo〕*n.* 大提琴

Look at the picture for question 8.

8. (**A**)　How does Jason feel?

　　A.　He feels cold.

　　B.　He feels hot.

　　C.　He feels thirsty.

　　* feel〔fil〕*v.* 覺得

　　　thirsty〔ˈθɝstɪ〕*adj.* 口渴的

Look at the picture for question 9.

9. (**B**)　What are they doing?

　　A.　They are playing.

　　B.　They are practicing kung-fu.

　　C.　They are acting.

　　* practice〔ˈpræktɪs〕*v.* 練習

　　　kung-fu 中國功夫　　act〔ækt〕*v.* 演戲

Look at the picture for question 10.

10. (**A**) What is the man doing?

A. He is washing the car.　　B. He is driving the car.

C. He is painting the car.

* wash〔waʃ〕v. 洗　　drive〔draɪv〕v. 開（車）

paint〔pent〕v. 油漆

第二部份

11. (**A**) What a beautiful day!

A. Yes, we're having great weather.

B. Thank you.

C. It was a gift from my mother.

* beautiful〔'bjutəfəl〕adj. 美好的

great〔gret〕adj. 很棒的　　weather〔'wɛðɚ〕n. 天氣

gift〔gɪft〕n. 禮物

12. (**B**) Please turn down the TV.

A. I don't, either.　　　　B. No problem.

C. I'll get it.

* ***turn down*** 轉小聲（↔ *turn up*）　***No problem*** . 沒問題。

I'll get it . 我來接電話；我來開門。

13. (**B**) How is your family?

A. He is fine, thank you.

B. They are all fine, thank you.

C. It's the best.

* family〔'fæməlɪ〕n. 家人

14. (**C**) Can you tell me the time?

    A. I could tell time when I was five years old.

    B. I will have some free time after lunch.

    C. Sorry, I don't have a watch either.

    * *Can you tell me the time?* 你可以告訴我現在幾點嗎？

      (= *Can you tell me what time it is?*)

    注意：time 前面一定要加定冠詞 the。

    tell time 看鐘錶；看時間   *free time* 空閒時間

15. (**A**) The school bell is ringing.

    A. Time to go to class.

    B. It's for you.

    C. Who's at the door?

    * bell (bɛl) *n.* 鐘；門鈴   ring (rɪŋ) *v.* (鐘、鈴) 響

16. (**C**) Have you seen my math book?

    A. My math book is blue.

    B. I'm not good at math either.

    C. It's on the desk.

    * math (mæθ) *n.* 數學   *be good at* 擅長

17. (**A**) What time do you get out of class?

    A. We go home at 4:30.

    B. I can get out of class when I am sick.

    C. I didn't get a lot out of that class.

    * *get out of class* 下課   *out of* 從… (= *from*)

18. (**A**) I love pizza. It's my favorite food.
       A. Mine, too.
       B. I also love food.   C. I'll have a medium.

     * 注意：A. 須改爲 Me, too. 才能選。
     pizza〔'pitsə〕n. 披薩   favorite〔'fevərɪt〕adj. 最喜愛的
     medium〔'midɪəm〕n. 中等尺寸的東西

19. (**C**) What would you like for dessert?
       A. I'd like some beef noodles.
       B. I'd never desert you.   C. Nothing for me, thanks.

     * dessert〔dɪ'zɝt〕n. 餐後甜點
     beef noodles 牛肉麵   desert〔dɪ'zɝt〕v. 拋棄

20. (**B**) How old is your sister?
       A. She is very tall and thin.
       B. She is sixteen.   C. She is fine.
     * thin〔θɪn〕adj. 瘦的

第三部份

21. (**C**) M：All aboard!
       W：Excuse me, conductor. When will we get to
          West Branch?
       M：This train doesn't stop at West Branch. You'll
          have to get off at Mill Town and take a shuttle
          bus from there.
       W：How long will that take?
       M：You should be in West Branch by 6:00.

Question: How will the woman get to West Branch?

A. She will change trains at Mill Town at 6:00.
B. She will take the 6:00 train to West Branch.
C. She will take a bus from Mill Town.

* aboard〔ə'bord〕 *adv.* 上（車、船、飛機）
  conductor〔kən'dʌktə〕 *n.* 列車長   ***get to*** 到達
  get off 下車   ***shuttle bus*** 近距離往返行駛的巴士
  take〔tek〕 *v.* 花費時間   change〔tʃendʒ〕 *v.* 換乘交通工具

22. (**A**) M: Excuse me, miss. Can I buy a glass of wine on
            this flight?
         W: Drinks are complimentary for all business class
            passengers, sir. There is no charge.
         M: In that case, I'll have a glass of red wine.
         W: Very well, sir. But I can't give it to you now.
            You'll have to wait until after takeoff.

         Question: Why won't the flight attendant give the man
                  a glass of wine?

         A. The plane is about to take off.
         B. There is no drinking allowed on the flight.
         C. He does not have enough money to pay for it.

         * wine〔waɪn〕 *n.* 葡萄酒   flight〔flaɪt〕 *n.* 班機
           drink〔drɪŋk〕 *n.* 飲料 *v.* 喝酒
           complimentary〔ˌkɑmplə'mɛntərɪ〕 *adj.* 免費的
           business class 商務艙   passenger〔'pæsndʒə〕 *n.* 乘客
           charge〔tʃɑrdʒ〕 *n.* 費用   ***in that case*** 那樣的話
           takeoff〔'tekˌɔf〕 *n.* 起飛   ***flight attendant*** 空服員
           be about to + V. 即將   ***take off*** 起飛
           allow〔ə'laʊ〕 *v.* 允許   ***pay for*** 付錢買

23. (**B**)　M：How about going to the movies this afternoon?

W：I'd love to, but I can't. I have to finish cleaning the house.

M：That's a lot of work! Why don't you ask your brother to help you?

W：He won't help me because it's my turn. He did the housework last week.

Question：Why won't the woman's brother help her do the housework?

A. He is going to the movies.

B. It's not his turn to do housework.

C. He has too much homework to do.

＊ ***How about + V-ing?*** 做～如何？

go to the movies 去看電影

finish + V-ing 完成　　clean〔klin〕*v.* 打掃

That's a lot of work. 那很費事！

it's one's turn 輪到某人做～

housework〔'haʊs,wɜk〕*n.* 家事

homework〔'hom,wɜk〕*n.* 家庭作業

24. (**B**)　W：Why are you so out of breath?

M：I just ran 10 blocks.

W：Why? Were you late for school?

M：No, I'm just trying to keep in shape.

Question : Why is the man out of breath?

A. He was late for school.

B. He was exercising.

C. He is out of shape.

* breath〔brɛθ〕n. 呼吸　　*out of breath* 上氣不接下氣的
  block〔blɑk〕n. 街區　　late〔let〕adj. 遲到的
  keep〔kip〕v. 保持　　*in shape* 身體狀況良好的
  exercise〔'ɛksɚ,saɪz〕v. 運動
  out of shape 身體狀況不佳的

25. (**A**)　W : Can you give me a hand with this box? It's heavy.

M : Sure. What's in it?

W : It's full of books.

M : Wow! You could open a bookstore!

Question : What does the woman want?

A. She wants the man to help her carry the books.

B. She wants to give the man some books.

C. She wants to open a bookstore.

* *give sb. a hand* 幫忙某人 (= *help sb.*)
  heavy〔'hɛvɪ〕adj. 重的　　*be full of* 充滿
  bookstore〔'buk,stor〕n. 書店 (= *bookshop*)
  carry〔'kærɪ〕v. 搬運

26. (**C**) W : Would you like to have dinner at my house on Friday?

M : Sure. How do I get there?

W : Start here on Central Avenue and turn left. Walk three blocks, then turn right and you'll see a park. My house is on the other side of the park.

M : Maybe you should draw a map for me. I don't want to get lost.

Question : Why does the man want the woman to draw a map?

A. He doesn't know where Central Avenue is.

B. He doesn't know how to draw a map.

C. He doesn't know where the woman's house is.

* avenue〔'ævə,nju〕*n.* 大街　***turn left*** 左轉
turn right 右轉　　side〔saɪd〕*n.* 邊　　draw〔drɔ〕*v.* 畫
map〔mæp〕*n.* 地圖　　***get lost*** 迷路

27. (**C**) M : How are we going to get to the concert tonight?

W : My brother will drive us. He just got his license.

M : Is he a good driver?

W : Sure. My parents trust him with their car.

Question : How will they get to the concert?

A. The woman will drive her parents' new car.

B. The man's parents will drive them.

C. The woman's brother will take them.

* concert〔'kɑnsɝt〕*n.* 音樂會
drive〔draɪv〕*v.* 開車送（某人）
license〔'laɪsṇs〕*n.* 駕照　　driver〔'draɪvɚ〕*n.* 駕駛人
trust〔trʌst〕*v.* 託付

28. (**A**)　W : What did the doctor say?

　　　　M : He said it's just a cold and to get plenty of rest.

　　　　W : Did he give you any medicine?

　　　　M : No.　He said I should feel better by tomorrow.

　　　Question : What should the man do?

　　　A.　He should take a rest.

　　　B.　He should take some medicine.

　　　C.　He should see a doctor tomorrow.

　　　* cold〔kold〕*n.* 感冒　　***plenty of*** 很多 (= *a lot of*)
　　　rest〔rɛst〕*n.* 休息　　medicine〔'mɛdəsn〕*n.* 藥
　　　by tomorrow 到了明天　　***take a rest*** 休息一下
　　　take〔tek〕*v.* 吃 (藥)

29. (**C**)　M : Have you heard the news?　John and Alice are
　　　　　　　getting married.

　　　　W : Really?　When is the big day?

　　　　M : They haven't decided yet.　He only asked her
　　　　　　last night.

　　　Question : What happened last night?

　　　A.　John and Alice got married.

　　　B.　John told the woman he will marry Alice.

　　　C.　John asked Alice to marry him.

　　　* ***get married*** 結婚　　big〔bɪg〕*adj.* 重大的
　　　decide〔dɪ'saɪd〕*v.* 決定　　happen〔'hæpən〕*v.* 發生
　　　marry〔'mærɪ〕*v.* 與…結婚　　***ask sb. to V.*** 要求某人~

30. (**C**) M : Have you decided what to major in at college?

W : Not yet. I'd like to study biology, but my parents hope I'll choose computer science.

M : I think you should study what you like. It's your life.

W : You don't know my parents.

Question : What does the man think the woman should do?

A. He thinks the woman should get to know his parents better.

B. He thinks the woman should study computer science.

C. He thinks the woman should major in biology.

* major〔'medʒɚ〕 v. 主修 < in >

college〔'kɑlɪdʒ〕 n. 大學　　***not yet*** 還沒

biology〔baɪ'ɑlədʒɪ〕 n. 生物學　　choose〔tʃuz〕 v. 選擇

computer science 電子計算機科學　　***get to V.*** 有機會做~

二、閱讀能力測驗

第一部份：詞彙和結構

1. (**B**) It took Peter a long time to find a job after he left school. <u>At</u> last, he found a job as a teacher.

彼得畢業後，花了很久的時間才找到工作。<u>最後</u>，他找到當老師的工作。

at last 最後 (= *in the end* = *finally*)

* job〔dʒɑb〕 n. 工作　　***leave school*** 畢業

as〔æz〕 *prep.* 擔任

2. (**C**) Mr. Brown <u>has gone</u> to America, so he isn't here now.
布朗先生<u>已經去</u>美國了，所以他現在人不在這裡。

$\begin{cases} \text{have gone to} \quad 已經去了 (去了未回) \\ \text{have been to} \quad 曾經去過 (去了又回) \end{cases}$

3. (**D**) It's <u>illegal</u> for people under 20 to drive a car in Taiwan.
在台灣，未滿二十歲的人開車是<u>違法的</u>。

(A) humid〔ˈhjumɪd〕 *adj.* 潮濕的
(B) active〔ˈæktɪv〕 *adj.* 主動的
(C) comfortable〔ˈkʌmfɚtəbḷ〕 *adj.* 舒服的
(D) ***illegal***〔ɪˈligḷ〕 *adj.* 違法的 (↔ *legal*)

4. (**D**) <u>On</u> Christmas Eve, we'll have a big dinner and then we'll go to church together.
在聖誕夜，我們將吃一頓豐盛的晚餐，然後一起上教堂。

表示特定日子的早、午、晚，介系詞用 on。

* ***Christmas Eve*** 聖誕夜　　***big***〔bɪg〕 *adj.* 豐盛的
go to church 上教堂；作禮拜

5. (**A**) Not only you but also I <u>am</u> right, so we don't have to fight about this.
不但你沒錯，我也沒錯，所以我們沒必要為這件事吵架。

not only A but also B「不但 A，而且 B」，做主詞時，
強調部份是 B，故動詞的單複數視 B 決定，故空格應填 I
的 be 動詞 ***am***，選 (A)。

* right〔raɪt〕 *adj.* 正確的　　fight〔faɪt〕 *v.* 吵架 < *about* >

6. (**B**) I have three brothers. One is a teacher, and <u>the others</u>
are businessmen.

我有三個兄弟。一個是老師，<u>另外兩個</u>是商人。

有限定三個人，排除掉一個人之後，剩下的那兩個人，
要加定冠詞 the。

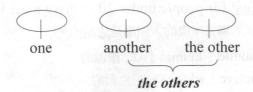

one　　　another　　　the other

the others

* businessman〔'bɪznɪsmən〕*n.* 商人

7. (**A**) There is a "No Parking" sign over there. Your car will
<u>be towed</u> away if you park your car there.

那邊有個「禁止停車」的告示牌。如果你把車子停在那裡，
你的車子將<u>被拖吊</u>。

tow away「拖吊」，按照句意爲被動語態，即「be 動詞＋
p.p.」的形式，故選 (A) ***be towed***。

* park〔pɑrk〕*v.* 停車　　sign〔saɪn〕*n.* 告示牌

8. (**C**) Christmas is coming, and everything in the department
store is <u>on</u> sale.

聖誕節快到了，百貨公司裡的每樣東西都在<u>特價</u>。

$\begin{cases} 商品＋be 動詞＋\textit{on sale} \quad （商品）特價 \\ 人或店家＋\textit{have a sale} \quad （人或店家）舉行特賣 \end{cases}$

* ***department store*** 百貨公司

9. (**C**) The shirts need <u>washing</u>, but you don't have to do it now.
襯衫需要<u>洗</u>了，但是你不用現在洗。

$$\begin{cases} \text{物} + \text{need} + \text{V-ing} \quad 需要 \\ = \text{物} + \text{need} + \text{to be p.p.} \end{cases}$$

本句可改為：The shirts need *to be washed*.

* shirt〔ʃɝt〕*n.* 襯衫

10. (**B**) Could you please stop <u>making</u> so much noise?　We are in a hospital, and the patients need some rest.
請你停止<u>製造</u>噪音，好嗎？這裡是醫院，病人需要休息。

$$\begin{cases} \text{stop} + \text{V-ing} \quad 停止（一個動作） \\ \text{stop} + \text{to V.} \quad 停下來，去做（二個動作） \end{cases}$$

* ***make noise*** 製造噪音　　hospital〔'hɑspɪtl̩〕*n.* 醫院
patient〔'peʃənt〕*n.* 病人

11. (**C**) There is a shortage of water because there has been very <u>little</u> rain recently.
因為最近雨下得<u>很少</u>，所以現在缺水。

$$\begin{cases} \text{few} + 可數名詞 \quad 少（指少到幾乎沒有，具否定意味） \\ \text{little} + 不可數名詞 \end{cases}$$

$$\begin{cases} \text{a few} + 可數名詞 \quad 一些（接近 some，具肯定意味） \\ \text{a little} + 不可數名詞 \end{cases}$$

rain 為不可數名詞，又按照句意，雨下得「非常少」，
故選 (C) ***little***。

* shortage〔'ʃɔrtɪdʒ〕*n.* 缺乏
recently〔'risn̩tlɪ〕*adv.* 最近

12. (**A**) I borrowed your pen without asking first, and I lost it.
I don't know <u>what</u> to do.

我沒事先問你，就拿了你的筆，並且把它弄丟了。我不知道
該怎辦。

I don't know ***what to do***. （我不知道該怎麼辦。）
I don't know ***how to do it***. （我不知道該如何做。）

* borrow〔'baro〕v. 借　　first〔fɜst〕adv. 先
without〔wɪð'aut〕prep. 沒有　　lose〔luz〕v. 遺失

13. (**C**) When he took off his hat, I <u>noticed</u> that he was bald.

當他脫下帽子時，我注意到他禿頭。

(A) produce〔prə'djus〕v. 生產；製造
(B) imagine〔ɪ'mædʒɪn〕v. 想像
(C) ***notice***〔'notɪs〕v. 注意到
(D) surprise〔sə'praɪz〕v. 使驚訝

* ***take off*** 脫掉（衣服、帽子等）（↔ ***put on***）
hat〔hæt〕n. 帽子　　bald〔bɔld〕adj. 禿頭的

14. (**B**) Matt : <u>How often</u> do you go to cram school?
Leo : Four times a week.

麥特：你多久去一次補習班？
里歐：一個禮拜四次。

(A) How many～？　～有多少？（問數量）
(B) ***How often***～？ ～多久一次？（問頻率）
(C) How long～？　～多長？；～多久？（問距離或時間）
(D) How old～？　～幾歲？（問年紀）

* ***cram school*** 補習班　　time〔taɪm〕n. 次數

15. (**B**) She looks only 30, but in fact she's much <u>older</u> than she looks. 她看起來只有三十歲，但實際上，她的實際年齡比她的外表<u>大</u>很多。

由 than 可知，空格應填一比較級，又 much 可修飾比較級，加強語氣，故選 (B) *older*。

* *in fact* 事實上　　look〔luk〕*v.* 看起來

第二部份：段落填空

Questions 16-20

Tina went to Taipei Zoo <u>on</u> January 25. It was her birthday.

          16

She got up early that day, and then she <u>met</u> her friends at the

                   17

MRT station. They spent twenty minutes <u>taking</u> the MRT.

                      18

<u>When</u> they got there, it started to rain. But they didn't want to

 19

give <u>up</u>. After a while, the rain stopped. They had a very good

    20

time on that day.

一月二十五日那天，蒂娜去台北動物園。那天是她的生日。她那天一大早就起床，到捷運站和朋友碰面。他們搭了二十分鐘的捷運。他們抵達那裡的時候，開始下起雨來。可是他們不想因此作罷。過了一會兒，雨就停了。那天他們玩得很開心。

zoo〔zu〕*n.* 動物園　　　***get up*** 起床

station〔'steʃən〕*n.* 車站　　start〔stɑrt〕*v.* 開始

while〔hwaɪl〕*n.* 一會兒　　***have a good time*** 玩得愉快

16. (**C**) **on** + 月份 + 日 在幾月幾日

17. (**D**) meet〔mit〕v. 會面，本篇敘述爲過去式，故選 (D) **met**。

18. (**B**) 人 + spend + 時間 + V-ing （人）花多久時間做～

19. (**C**) 按照句意，「當」他們到那裡之後，開始下雨，故選 (C) **When**。
(A) Although「雖然」，(B) Because「因爲」，(D) If「如果」，
均不合句意。

20. (**A**) **give up** 放棄

Questions 21-25

Chinese New Year is a special holiday for everyone. At that
time, family members <u>from</u> all over Taiwan get together. They
                      21
<u>enjoy</u> talking, eating, and having a good time.
  22

農曆新年對每個人來說，都是個很特別的假日。農曆新年期間，散
佈在台灣各地的家族成員會團聚在一起。他們喜歡聊天及吃東西，度過
一段開心的時光。

> ***Chinese New Year*** 中國農曆新年
> special〔'spɛʃəl〕adj. 特別的   member〔'mɛmbɚ〕n. 成員
> ***all over*** 遍及   ***get together*** 聚集

Older family members talk about work and friends. They
share news of the last year. Younger people have fun <u>playing</u>.
                                                         23
They also get red envelopes with "lucky money" inside.

老一輩的家族成員會談論工作和朋友。他們會分享去年所發生的點點滴滴。年輕人玩得很高興。他們也會拿到裡面裝有「壓歲錢」的紅包袋。

> ***talk about*** 談論　　share〔ʃɛr〕*v.* 分享
> envelope〔'ɛnvə,lop〕*n.* 信封　　***red envelope*** 紅包
> lucky〔'lʌkɪ〕*adj.* 幸運的　　***lucky money*** 壓歲錢
> inside〔'ɪn'saɪd〕*adv.* 在裡面

It's also a time to welcome the new year. People clean their houses. Friends visit each other. And people <u>wish</u> each other
24
good luck.

此時也是迎接新年的時候。人們忙著打掃房子。朋友相互拜訪。而且大家也會互道恭喜。

> welcome〔'wɛlkəm〕*v.* 歡迎　　visit〔'vɪzɪt〕*v.* 拜訪
> ***each other*** 彼此　　luck〔lʌk〕*n.* 運氣

There's probably only one <u>terrible</u> thing about Chinese
25
New Year: traffic. People say that on some days, the road from Keelung to Kaohsiung is like the world's biggest parking lot!

關於農曆春節，大概只有一件可怕的事情，那就是交通問題。在這段期間有幾天，大家都說，從基隆到高雄這段路，就像是全世界最大的停車場！

> probably〔'prɑbəblɪ〕*adv.* 大概　　traffic〔'træfɪk〕*n.* 交通
> ***parking lot*** 停車場

21.(**D**) 介系詞 ***from*** 表「從～（地方）來」。

22. (**A**) (A) *enjoy* 〔 ɪn'dʒɔɪ 〕 v. 喜歡；享受（後接動名詞）
          (B) plan 〔 plæn 〕 v. 計畫（後接不定詞）
          (C) want 〔 wɑnt 〕 v. 想要（後接不定詞）
          (D) hate 〔 het 〕 v. 討厭（句意不合）

23. (**C**) *have fun* + *V-ing* 做～很愉快

24. (**B**) (A) hope 〔 hop 〕 v. 希望（不可接人稱受詞）
          (B) *wish* 〔 wɪʃ 〕 v. 祝福
          (C) speak 〔 spik 〕 v. 說（語言）
          (D) say 〔 se 〕 v. 說（不及物動詞）

25. (**D**) 按照句意，「不好的」事情，選 (D) *terrible* 〔'tɛrəbl̩〕 adj.
          糟糕的。

第三部份：閱讀理解

Question 26

誠徵

➢ 男性，三十歲以下

➢ 精通英文

➢ 一年教學經驗

☎ 2876-5432   白先生

wanted 〔'wɑntɪd〕 adj. 徵求⋯的   male 〔 mel 〕 n. 男性
command 〔 kə'mænd 〕 n.（對語言的）運用自如的能力；精通
experience 〔 ɪk'spɪrɪəns 〕 n. 經驗

26. (**A**) 懷特先生想徵求什麼人？

(A) 老師。　　　(B) 祕書。　　　(C) 歌手。　　　(D) 廚師。

* secretary〔'sɛkrə,tɛrɪ〕n. 祕書
  singer〔'sɪŋɚ〕n. 歌手　　　cook〔kʊk〕n. 廚師

Questions 27-28

A	B
屋齡三十二年 三房，兩衛 兩廳，一間廚房 售十八萬元 二千平方英呎	屋齡十年 三房，一衛 兩廳，一間廚房 售十七萬元 一千四百五十平方英呎
C	D
屋齡十二年 二房，一衛 一廳，一間廚房 售十六萬五千元 一千六百五十四平方英呎	屋齡二十五年 四房，兩衛 兩廳，二間廚房 售二十八萬元 三千一百平方英呎

bdrm 臥室（= *bedroom*）　　　ba 浴室（= *bathroom*）
lvrm 客廳（= *living room*）　　　ktch 廚房（= *kitchen*）
sq. ft 平方英呎（= *square feet*）

27. (**C**) 哪一間房子是在西元一九九〇年建造的？

（西元）2002 −（西元）1990 = 12（年屋齡）

* build〔bɪld〕v. 興建

28. (**D**) 懷特夫婦有三個小孩。他們要買一間房子供全家人住。他們
想讓每個小孩各自有自己的房間。哪間房子最適合他們？

懷特夫婦共用一間房間,再加上三個小孩各自有自己的一間
房間,總共需要四間臥室,故選 (D)。

Questions 29-30

生 日 派 對

史考提‧懷特受邀在一月一日,星期六,參加葛瑞思‧布朗
十四歲的生日派對。派對將在晚上六點鐘開始,九點半結束。
舉行地點於天母西路 252 號。請來電:2871-8125。週六見。

---

invite〔ɪnˈvaɪt〕v. 邀請　　conclude〔kənˈklud〕v. 結束
hold〔hold〕v. 舉行

29. (**B**) 這派對將舉行多久？

(A) 二小時。　　　　　　(B) 三小時。
(C) 無法得知。　　　　　(D) 不到四個小時。

30. (**B**) 派對的地點在哪裡？

(A) 在客廳。　　　　　　(B) 無法得知。
(C) 在工廠。　　　　　　(D) 在廚房。

* factory〔ˈfæktrɪ〕n. 工廠

Questions 31-33

Many people think the English do not like to speak other languages. In fact, English is a mixture of words from many different languages. Because of this, the vocabulary of the English language is very large. It is much larger than that of almost every other language in the world.

很多人認為英國人不喜歡說其它語言。事實上，英語是很多不同語言的混合體。因此，英語的字彙量非常龐大。比世界上幾乎所有的其它語言，字彙量還大。

> ***the English*** 英國人 (視為複數，故接複數動詞)
> language〔'læŋgwɪdʒ〕 *n.* 語言　　mixture〔'mɪkstʃɚ〕 *n.* 混合
> different〔'dɪfrənt〕 *adj.* 不同的　　***because of*** + *N.* 因為
> vocabulary〔və'kæbjə,lɛrɪ〕 *n.* 字彙
> large〔lɑrdʒ〕 *adj.* 多的　　***in the world*** 在全世界

Many English words come from Latin, the old language of Rome, and also from ancient Greek. From Latin we get words like "wine," "use" and "day." From Greek we have words such as "photograph," "Bible" and "ink." Because these two languages are dead, the words have most often come through other languages such as French, or the old German languages. There are also many words from both Greek and Latin together—"television," for example. Here "tele" is Greek for "far" and "vision" comes from Latin and means "seeing."

很多英文字來自拉丁文，即羅馬時代使用的古文字，和古希臘文。源自拉丁文的字，例如 wine，use 和 day。而源自希臘文的字，例如 photograph，Bible 和 ink。因為這兩種語言都已經不再使用了，所以通

常透過法文或古德文而流傳下來。也有很多字是源自於拉丁文及希臘文的，例如 television。tele 在希臘文是「遠」的意思，而 vision 則是拉丁文「看」的意思。

come from 起源於   Latin〔ˋlætɪn〕n. 拉丁文
Rome〔rom〕n. 羅馬 (古羅馬帝國的首都)
ancient〔ˋenʃənt〕adj. 古代的   Greek〔grik〕n. 希臘文
wine〔waɪn〕n. 葡萄酒   such as 例如
photograph〔ˋfotəˏɡræf〕n. 照片   Bible〔ˋbaɪbḷ〕n. 聖經
ink〔ɪŋk〕n. 墨水   dead〔dɛd〕adj. (語言) 不再使用的
French〔frɛntʃ〕n. 法文   German〔ˋdʒɝmən〕adj. 德國的
for example 例如

31. (**C**) 在古代，羅馬人是說哪一種語言？

(A) 英文。　　　　　　　(B) 法文。

(C) 拉丁文。　　　　　　(D) 希臘文。

　　* times〔taɪmz〕n. pl. (特定的) 時代；時期
　　　Roman〔ˋromən〕n. 羅馬人

32. (**A**) 為什麼英文字彙量很大？

(A) 因為英文本身就從很多不同的語言轉借許多字。

(B) 因為英文是歷史最悠久的語言。

(C) 因為英文是大多數人使用的語言。

(D) 因為英文是活的語言。

　　* borrow〔ˋbaro〕v. (從外語) 轉借 < from >
　　　history〔ˋhɪstrɪ〕n. 歷史
　　　living〔ˋlɪvɪŋ〕adj. (語言) 在使用的 (↔ dead)

33. (**C**) 英文字 "television" 源自什麼語言？

    (A) 拉丁文。   (B) 希臘文。

    (C) <u>拉丁文及希臘文。</u> (D) 德文。

Question 34-35

I was busy looking for two free tickets to a rock concert when my little sister Lisa came into my room. She wanted to tell me something but I was not interested. I pushed her out and closed the door behind her. Twenty minutes later, I gave up and called Jimmy. "Jimmy, I'm sorry that we can't go to the concert tonight. I've lost the tickets." Jimmy angrily hung up the phone and I felt very upset. Later that evening, Lisa handed me the concert tickets I had lost. "I wanted to give them to you, but you were so angry. I found them at your door, so I think they're yours, right? Are you still angry now?" she asked. "It's too late. But never mind. Thank you, anyway," I answered weakly.

當我妹妹麗莎進我的房間找我的時候，我正忙著找那兩張搖滾演唱會的免費門票。她好像有事情要跟我說，不過我沒興趣。我把她推出房門，把門關上。二十分鐘後，我放棄找票，打電話給吉米。「吉米，很抱歉，我們今晚不能去演唱會了。我把票弄丟了。」吉米生氣地掛斷電話，我覺得很生氣。當晚晚一點的時候，麗莎把我遺失的門票交給我。「我本來想早點給你的，但是你太生氣了。我是在你的房門口找到門票的，所以我想那是你的，對不對？你現在還在生氣嗎？」她問道。「來不及了。不過算了。無論如何，**謝謝妳，**」我有氣無力地回答。

be busy + *V-ing* 忙著做～　　*look for* 尋找

free〔fri〕*adj.* 免費的　　ticket〔'tɪkɪt〕*n.* 入場券

rock〔rɑk〕*n.* 搖滾樂　　concert〔'kɑnsɝt〕*n.* 演唱會

little sister 妹妹　　interested〔'ɪntrɪstɪd〕*adj.* 有興趣的

push〔puʃ〕*v.* 推　　behind〔bɪ'haɪnd〕*prep.* 在…的後面

later〔'letɚ〕*adv.* 後來　　*give up* 放棄

sorry〔'sɔrɪ〕*adj.* 感到抱歉的；感到遺憾的

tonight〔tə'naɪt〕*adv.* 在今晚

angrily〔'æŋgrɪlɪ〕*adv.* 生氣地　　*hang up* 掛斷（電話）

phone〔fon〕*n.* 電話（= *telephone*）

upset〔ʌp'sɛt〕*adj.* 心煩的；不高興的

hand〔hænd〕*v.* 拿給　　*never mind* 沒關係

anyway〔'ɛnɪˌwe〕*adv.* 無論如何；不管怎樣

weakly〔'wiklɪ〕*adv.* 微弱地

34. (**D**) 麗莎在哪裡找到那兩張門票的？

　　(A) 在客廳。　　　　　　　(B) 在廚房。

　　(C) 在浴室門口。　　　　　(D) <u>在作者的房門口。</u>

　　* writer〔'raɪtɚ〕*n.* 作者

35. (**C**) 何者為真？

　　(A) 吉米很高興得知發生了什麼事。

　　(B) 作者和吉米最後去了演唱會。

　　(C) <u>麗莎找到門票，並且把門票交給作者。</u>

　　(D) 吉米找到門票。

　　* true〔tru〕*adj.* 真實的；正確的

　　　at last 最後

三、寫作能力測驗

第一部份：單句寫作

第 1～5 題：句子改寫

1. Bob　：Did you remember to feed the dog?
   Sarah : Yes, I did.
   Sarah remembered _____.

   重點結構：「remember + V-ing」的用法

   　解　答：<u>Sarah remembered feeding the dog.</u>

   句型分析：主詞 + remember + V-ing

   　說　明：「記得做過某件事」用 remember + V-ing，此題
   　　　　　　須在 remember 之後加動名詞，表示已經做了某件
   　　　　　　事情，並且記得。

   ＊ feed〔fid〕v. 餵

2. Watching American movies on TV helps me learn English.
   It _____.

   重點結構：以 It 為虛主詞引出的句子

   　解　答：<u>It helps me learn English to watch American
   　　　　　　movies on TV.</u>

   句型分析：It + 動詞 + to V.

   　說　明：虛主詞 it 代替不定詞片語，不定詞片語則擺在句尾，
   　　　　　　故 watching American movies on TV 改為 to
   　　　　　　watch American movies on TV。

3. Amy played basketball with her friends.
   When _____?

　　重點結構：過去式的 wh-問句

　　解　　答：<u>When did Amy play basketball with her friends?</u>

　　句型分析：When + did + 主詞 + 原形動詞？

　　說　　明：這一題應將過去式直述句改為 wh-問句，除了要加
　　　　　　　助動詞 did，還要記得助動詞後的動詞須用原形動
　　　　　　　詞，因此 played 要改成 play。

4. How does Joseph go to school?
   I don't know _____.

　　重點結構：間接問句做名詞子句

　　解　　答：<u>I don't know how Joseph goes to school.</u>

　　句型分析：I don't know + how + 主詞 + 動詞

　　說　　明：在 wh-問句前加 I don't know，形成間接問句，必
　　　　　　　須把動詞 go 放在最後面，又因主詞 Joseph 為第三
　　　　　　　人稱單數，go 須加 es，並把問號改成句點。

5. Jason cleaned the classroom.（用被動式）
   The classroom _____.

　　重點結構：被動語態字序

　　解　　答：<u>The classroom was cleaned by Jason.</u>

　　句型分析：主詞 + be 動詞 + 過去分詞 + by + 受詞

　　說　　明：一般被動語態的結構是「主詞 + be 動詞 + 過去
　　　　　　　分詞」，按照句意為過去式，又 The classroom
　　　　　　　為第三人稱單數，所以 be 動詞用 was。

第 6～10 題：句子合併

6. Megan asked Carrie something. (用 why)
Mark was late for school today.

_____

重點結構：名詞子句當受詞用

解　　答：<u>Megan asked Carrie why Mark was late for school today.</u>

句型分析：主詞＋動詞＋why＋主詞＋動詞

說　　明：Megan 要問 Carrie 一件事情，這件事就是關於 Mark 今天上學遲到的事情，兩句之間用 why 來合併。若是直接問句，則 Megan 問 Carrie, "Why was Mark late for school today?"，現在要改為間接問句，即「疑問詞＋主詞＋動詞」的形式，在 Megan asked Carrie 後面接 why Mark was late for school today，並把問號改為句點。

7. We visited Boston.
We visited New York. (用 both…and～)

_____

重點結構：both A and B 的用法

解　　答：<u>We visited both Boston and New York.</u>

句型分析：主詞＋動詞＋both＋名詞＋and＋名詞

說　　明：句意是「我們不但遊覽了波士頓，還有紐約」，用「both…and～」合併兩個受詞，表「不僅…而且～」。

* visit〔ˈvɪzɪt〕v. 參觀

8. The TV program is exciting.
   Danny watches the TV program again. (用 enough)

   _____.

   重點結構：enough 的用法

   解　答：The TV program is exciting enough for Danny
   　　　　to watch again.

   句型分析：主詞＋be 動詞＋形容詞＋enough＋for＋受詞＋
   　　　　to V.

   説　明：這題的意思是說「這電視節目夠刺激，所以丹尼再看
   　　　　一遍」，副詞 enough「足夠地」須置於形容詞之後，
   　　　　「足以～」則以不定詞表示。

   ＊ program〔'progræm〕n. 節目
   　exciting〔ɪk'saɪtɪŋ〕adj. 刺激的

9. Here is a magazine.
   I enjoy the magazine very much. (用 which)

   _____.

   重點結構：由 which 引導的形容詞子句

   解　答：Here is a magazine which I enjoy very much.

   句型分析：Here is a magazine＋which＋主詞＋動詞

   説　明：句意是「這是一本我很愛看的雜誌」，在合併兩句
   　　　　時，用 which 代替先行詞 a magazine，引導形容
   　　　　詞子句，在子句中做受詞。

   ＊ magazine〔ˌmægə'zin〕n. 雜誌

10. The farmer sold fruit.

The farmer made a lot of money. (用 by)

_____.

重點結構：「by + V-ing」的用法

解　答：The farmer made a lot of money by selling fruit.

句型分析：The farmer made a lot of money + by + 動名詞

説　明：這題的意思是說「這位農夫靠賣水果賺了很多錢」，用「by + V-ing」，表「藉由~（方法）」。

* fruit〔frut〕n. 水果
  make money 賺錢

第 11~15 題：重組

11. Children _____.

presents / mothers / on / their / buy / Mother's Day

重點結構：「buy + sb. + sth.」的用法

解　答：Children buy their mothers presents on Mother's Day.

句型分析：buy + 間接受詞（人）+ 直接受詞（物）

説　明：「買東西給某人」有兩種寫法：「buy + sb. + sth.」或「buy + sth. + for + sb.」，由於所列出的單字中沒有 for，這題重組只能用第一種寫法，又「on + 特定日子」，置於句尾，形成此句。

* present〔'prɛznt〕n. 禮物

12. Here _____.

the / comes / bus

重點結構：Here 置於句首的用法

解　答：<u>Here comes the bus.</u>

句型分析：Here ＋ 動詞 ＋ 主詞（一般名詞）

説　明：這題的意思是說「公車來了」，原本是 The bus comes here. Here 置於句首為加強語氣的用法，若主詞為一般名詞時，須與動詞倒裝。

13. Tina _____.

studied / two / for / English / has / years

重點結構：現在完成式字序

解　答：<u>Tina has studied English for two years.</u>

句型分析：主詞 ＋ have/has ＋ 過去分詞

説　明：一般現在完成式的結構是「主詞 ＋ have/has ＋ 過去分詞」，而「for ＋ 一段時間」，表「持續（多久）」，此時間片語通常置於句尾。

14. Peter asked Jean _____.

she / a / boyfriend / had / whether

重點結構：whether 的用法

解　答：<u>Peter asked Jean whether she had a boyfriend.</u>

句型分析：Peter asked Jean ＋ whether ＋ 主詞 ＋ 動詞 ＋ 受詞

説　明：whether 引導名詞子句，做動詞 asked 的受詞，表「是否」。

* boyfriend (ˈbɔɪˌfrɛnd) *n.* 男朋友

15. Jimmy _____.

such / everyone / a / boy / him / handsome / loves / is / that

重點結構：「such…that」的用法

解　答：<u>Jimmy is such a handsome boy that everyone</u>
<u>loves him.</u>

句型分析：主詞 + be 動詞 + such + 名詞 + that + 主詞 + 動詞

說　明：這題的意思是說「吉米長得很帥，所以每個人都喜
歡他」，合併兩句時，用「such…that～」，表
「如此…以致於～」。

* handsome〔'hænsəm〕adj. 英俊的

第二部份：段落寫作

題目：　今天是除夕夜，你／妳許下新年新希望，請根據圖片內容寫
　　　　一篇約 50 字的簡短描述。

　　I always make some resolutions *on Chinese New Year's Eve*. I want to be healthier, kinder and happier *next year*. *So* I promise to exercise more and to stay away from fast food. I *also* promise to be kind to everyone that I meet. I will try to help other people as much as I can. *Finally*, I promise to smile more *next year*. With a smile on my face, I can be happy and make other people happy, too. I hope I can keep my resolutions this year.

resolution〔ˌrɛzə'luʃən〕*n.* 決心要做的事

Chinese New Year's Eve 中國農曆新年除夕夜

healthy〔'hɛlθɪ〕*adj.* 健康的　　kind〔kaɪnd〕*adj.* 親切的

promise〔'prɑmɪs〕*v.* 答應；保證

exercise〔'ɛksə͵saɪz〕*v.* 運動

stay away from 遠離 (= *keep away from*)　　***fast food*** 速食

as much as *one can* 儘量 (= *as much as possible*)

smile〔smaɪl〕*v. n.* 微笑

keep a resolution 做到決心要做的事

全民英語能力分級檢定測驗
初級測驗 ③

一、聽力測驗

本測驗分三部份,全為三選一之選擇題,每部份各 10 題,共 30 題,作答時間約 20 分鐘。

第一部份： 看圖辨義

本部份共 10 題,試題冊上每題有一個圖片,請聽錄音機播出一個相關的問題,與 A、B、C 三個英語敘述後,選一個與所看到圖片最相符的答案,並在答案紙上相對的圓圈內塗黑作答。每題播出一遍,問題及選項均不印在試題冊上。

例： （看）

NT$80   NT$50

（聽）

Look at the picture.   How much is the hamburger?

A.   It's eighty dollars.
B.   It's fifty-five dollars.
C.   It's eighteen dollars.

正確答案為 A

Question 1

Question 2

Question 3

Question 4

Question 5

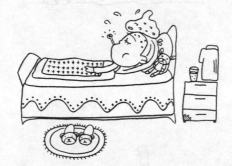

Question 6

請翻頁 ⟹

Question 7

Question 8

Question 9

Question 10

第二部份：問答

本部份共 10 題，每題錄音機會播出一個問句或直述句，每題播出一次，聽後請從試題冊上 A、B、C 三個選項中，選出一個最適合的回答或回應，並在答案紙上塗黑作答。

例：

（聽） Good morning, Kevin. How are you?

（看） A. I'm fine, thank you.
　　　 B. I'm in the living room.
　　　 C. My name is Kevin.

正確答案為 A

11. A. Chicken and rice.
　　 B. It's at 12:00.
　　 C. Thanks, but I'm not hungry.

12. A. I will see him tomorrow.
　　 B. I see him every day.
　　 C. I saw him this morning.

13. A. I haven't.
　　 B. I won't.
　　 C. I didn't.

14. A. I think I saw it last week.
　　 B. It was wonderful!
　　 C. I saw it with my brother.

15. A. Yes, I like it very
much.
B. Yes, you do.
C. Yes, it's a good day
to go swimming.

16. A. I reported it
yesterday.
B. No, I haven't.
C. Yes, I do.

17. A. Yes, it does.
B. Yes, it is.
C. No, it's not.

18. A. Since twelve o'clock.
B. You have to stand in
line.
C. I can't wait to see the
doctor.

19. A. Yes, I like to pet the dog.
B. Yes, and I have a dog.
C. I like dogs more than
cats.

20. A. Yes, isn't it beautiful?
B. Be careful.
C. I slipped it this morning.

請 翻 頁 ▷

第三部份：　簡短對話

本部份共 10 題，每題錄音機會播出一段對話及一個相關的問題，每題播出兩次，聽後請從試題冊上 A、B、C 三個選項中，選出一個最適合的回答，並在答案紙上塗黑作答。

例：

（聽）(Woman)　Good afternoon, ...Mr. Davis?

　　　(Man)　　Yes. I have an appointment with Dr. Sanders at two o'clock. My son Tommy has a fever.

　　　(Woman)　Oh, that's too bad. Well, please have a seat, Mr. Davis. Dr. Sanders will be right with you.

　　　Question:　Where did this conversation take place?

（看）A.　In a post office.

　　　B.　In a restaurant.

　　　C.　In a doctor's office.

正確答案為 C

21. A. The VCR is broken.
    B. She has to plug the cassette in, not insert it.
    C. The VCR has no power.

22. A. They will give it to a police officer.
    B. They will send it back to the owner.
    C. They will sell the wallet and send the money to the owner.

23. A. He is afraid to go by himself.
    B. There are no tickets left.
    C. There are only two seats left, and he needs six.

24. A. He is better at geography than math.
    B. He failed the geography test because that is a difficult subject for him.
    C. He wishes that Professor Brown taught math.

25. A. He saw a big typhoon today.
    B. The newspaper hasn't come yet.
    C. A typhoon is coming.

26. A. Help him carry the box.
    B. Tell him where the post office is.
    C. Give the box to his brother.

請 翻 頁 ⫸

27. A. He wants to buy
       some ice cream.
    B. He wants to know
       where Aisle 12 is.
    C. He wants to freeze
       some food.

28. A. In front of a window.
    B. In a restaurant.
    C. At a gas station.

29. A. He likes all of his
       classes.
    B. He doesn't like any
       of his classes.
    C. Math is his least
       favorite class.

30. A. Give the man a
       hamburger.
    B. Give the man a Coke.
    C. Order a number two
       meal instead.

二、閱讀能力測驗

本測驗分三部份，全為四選一之選擇題，共 35 題，作答時間 35 分鐘。

第一部份：　詞彙和結構

本部份共 15 題，每題含一個空格。請就試題冊上 A、B、C、D 四個選項中選出最適合題意的字或詞，標示在答案紙上。

1. Maggie closed her eyes and made a _____.
   A. wish
   B. cake
   C. tea
   D. coffee

2. I'm sorry for breaking your glasses. It's all my _____.
   A. joke
   B. question
   C. fault
   D. idea

3. Linda is very _____ after her holiday in Thailand, because the sun there is very hot.
   A. yellow
   B. black
   C. brown
   D. orange

請翻頁 ⫸

4. I feel it is great to take _____ in the hot springs
   in Yangmingshan.
   A. a bath
   B. a trip
   C. medicine
   D. an interest

5. Paul : I'm going to the Taipei City Hall. Bus Number
         286 goes there, _____?
   Rita : Yes, but you can take the MRT, too.
   A. does it
   B. doesn't it
   C. is it
   D. isn't it

6. George was _____ his new bicycle to his classmates
   this morning, but he found that his bicycle had been stolen
   after school.
   A. taking off
   B. showing off
   C. waiting for
   D. laughing at

7. Mike and I _____ all night decorating our new house.
   A took
   B spent
   C cost
   D paid

8. Tim is an active language learner. He always carries a
_____ with him.
A. story
B. dictionary
C. conversation
D. sentence

9. Stop _____! What a terrible voice you have!
A. singing
B. to sing
C. and sing
D. to singing

10. Melissa : Mom, I got the best grade on the English
test today.
Mother : Good job, daughter. I'm _____ of you.
A. sick
B. tired
C. sure
D. proud

11. Nancy _____ fake CDs when the police came.
A. sells
B. has sold
C. is selling
D. was selling

請 翻 頁

12. With e-mails and telephones, _____ has become easier, and the world is getting smaller.
    A. difference
    B. communication
    C. software
    D. housework

13. Fred and Jack are good friends, and _____ are basketball fans.
    A. all of them
    B. one of them
    C. both of them
    D. some of them

14. My father came into the kitchen to see what was _____.
    A. bad
    B. right
    C. wrong
    D. long

15. (In the teachers' office)
    Miss Ho : Mr. Ma, _____ students in the classroom?
    Mr. Ma : I don't think so. School is over.
    Miss Ho : But I hear people talking over there.
    A. are they
    B. do they
    C. is there
    D. are there

第二部份：段落填空

　　本部份共10題，包括二個段落，每個段落各含5個空格。
請就試題冊上A、B、C、D四個選項中選出最適合題意
的字或詞，標示在答案紙上。

Questions 16-20

Learning English ___(16)___ an interesting thing. It's just ___(17)___ playing basketball. First, we have to memorize new words. If we don't understand ___(18)___, we have to ___(19)___ in the dictionary. And then we have to practice ___(20)___ we can. If we don't miss any chance to do these things, our English will get better and better.

16. A. has
　　B. have
　　C. are
　　D. is

17. A. as
　　B. like
　　C. same
　　D. and

18. A. it
　　B. which
　　C. them
　　D. what

19. A. look at them
　　B. look them at
　　C. look up them
　　D. look them up

20. A. as often as
　　B. as well as
　　C. as seldom as
　　D. as quick as

請翻頁 ▯▯▯⇒

Questions 21-25

In the south of Taiwan, there is a very special place. ___(21)___ great weather, and beautiful forests. That place is Kenting National Park. Every year, millions of people ___(22)___. They come from all over Taiwan. People go there on honeymoons, school trips, and short weekend ___(23)___. Also, tourists from other countries love to visit the park.

At Kenting, ___(24)___. You can play in the water and relax on the beach. You can also visit the beautiful gardens and ___(25)___ the strange rocks with funny shapes. They have names like "frog rock" and "sail rock."

21. A. It's not expensive
    B. People are all friendly
    C. It has clean beaches,
    D. You can see snow,

22. A. visit the park
    B. worry about the beach
    C. go to Taipei
    D. stay at home

23. A. days
    B. jobs
    C. holidays
    D. sleep

24. A. it's boring
    B. there is a lot to do
    C. you don't have fun
    D. there is nothing to do

25. A. eat
    B. look at
    C. make
    D. understand

第三部份：閱讀理解

本部份共 10 題，包括數段短文，每段短文後有 1～3 個相關問題，請就試題冊上 A、B、C、D 四個選項中選出最適合者，標示在答案紙上。

Questions 26-27

Joseph and Nina are walking in a park.

Nina　　: You threw your garbage on the ground. Pick it up.

Joseph : Why? It's only a small bag. Anyway, it's empty.

Nina　　: We have to keep the park clean.

Joseph : But a lot of people do <u>the same thing</u>.

Nina　　: I know. Those people are wrong.

26. Nina
    A. threw something on the ground.
    B. cares about the park.
    C. agrees with Joseph.
    D. did something wrong.

27. What is <u>the same thing</u>?
    A. Walk in the park.
    B. Pick up their garbage.
    C. Keep the park clean.
    D. Throw garbage on the ground.

請翻頁 ▯▯▯▯⟹

Questions 28-30

　　Many people have the wrong idea about pigs. In fact, pigs are very clean animals. On farms, they live in dirty places, so they become very dirty. <u>In the wild</u>, pigs keep very clean.

　　They are also really smart. They may be smarter than dogs. So, pigs can learn things from people. Pigs are very friendly animals. Some people raise them as pets. Of course, people raise the small kind, not the big kind. Small pigs are very cute and they don't break things in the house. Big pigs usually live outside on farms, not in people's houses.

28. Pigs are _____.
　　A. dirty and stupid　　　　　B. shy and strange
　　C. dangerous and unfriendly　D. smart and gentle

29. What does "in the wild" in line three mean?
　　A. In nature.　　　　　　　　B. On farms.
　　C. Going crazy.　　　　　　　D. In people's houses.

30. Which of the following is true?
　　A. Pigs like to be dirty.
　　B. Only farmers raise pigs.
　　C. Dogs are smarter than pigs.
　　D. Some people raise small pigs in their houses.

<u>Questions 31-32</u>

This is a TV schedule. Read this and answer the questions.

Time	Program
7:00	Weather Report
7:30	Happy English
8:00	World News
9:00	Fashion News

31. Sarah wants to go to the beach with her friends tomorrow.
    What time should she watch TV to know whether it will
    rain or not?
    A. 7:00
    B. 7:30
    C. 8:00
    D. 9:00

32. Peter wants to know what's happening around the world,
    so what time should he turn on the TV?
    A. 7:00
    B. 7:30
    C. 8:00
    D. 9:00

請 翻 頁 ▯▭▭▷

Questions 33-35

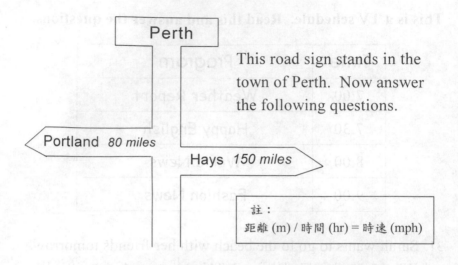

This road sign stands in the town of Perth. Now answer the following questions.

註：
距離 (m) / 時間 (hr) = 時速 (mph)

33. Laura is driving from Perth to Portland. She's driving at 40 miles per hour (mph). She left Perth at two in the afternoon. What time will she get to Portland?

    A. 3:30

    B. 3:00

    C. 4:00

    D. 4:30

34. Casper is driving to Hays from Perth. He's driving at 50 mph. He will stop for two hours for a show on the way. He left Perth at 10:00. What time will he get to Hays?
    A. 12:00
    B. 13:00
    C. 14:00
    D. 15:00

35. Linda is going to her friend's party in Portland. The party will begin at seven in the evening. She wants to get there 30 minutes early. If she drives at 40 mph, what time should she leave Perth?
    A. 5:30
    B. 4:30
    C. 5:00
    D. 4:00

請 翻 頁 ||⟹

三、寫作能力測驗

　　本測驗共有兩部份，第一部份為單句寫作，第二部份為段落寫作。測驗時間為 40 分鐘。

第一部份： 單句寫作

　　　　　　請將答案寫在寫作能力測驗答案紙對應的題號旁，如有拼字、標點、大小寫之錯誤，將予扣分。

第 1～5 題：句子改寫

　　　　　　請依題目之提示，將原句改寫成指定型式，並將改寫的句子完整地寫在答案紙上（包括提示之文字及標點符號）。

1. Getting a lot of lucky money is a happy thing.

　　It's _____.

2. I made my dog sit down.

　　My dog _____ by me.

3. I will never forget the good time we spent together.

　　Never _____.

4. It rains a lot in winter in Taipei.

　　We _____.

5. I spent two hours cleaning my bedroom.

　　It _____.

第 6～10 題：句子合併

　　　　請依照題目指示，將兩句合併成一句，並將合併的句子
　　　　完整地寫在答案紙上（包括提示之文字及標點符號）。

6. Study hard. （用 and）
   You will get good grades.

   _____.

7. I want to know the girl. （用 with 合併）
   That girl has short hair.

   _____.

8. The coffee is very hot. （用 so…that 合併）
   I can't drink it.

   _____.

9. I didn't see you yesterday. （用 either 合併）
   I didn't see you the day before yesterday.

   I didn't _____, and I didn't _____.

10. A man wants to see you. （用 who 合併）
    The man is called Dr. Wang.

    A man who _____.

請 翻 頁 ▯▯▯➡

第 11～15 題：重組

請將題目中所有提示字詞整合成一有意義的句子，並將重組的句子完整地寫在答案紙上（包括提示之文字及標點符號）。答案中必須使用所有提示字詞，且不能隨意增加字詞，否則不予計分。

11. What _____?

she / usually / does / do / Sundays / on

12. Would _____?

kind / to give / a / enough / you / me / be / hand

13. I _____.

to / frightened / too / open / my / am / eyes

14. Our teacher _____.

how / teaches / to / us / sing / songs / English

15. It _____.

must / frightening / to / a ghost / be / see

第二部份：段落寫作

題目： 昨天妳/你和姐姐及她的男朋友去看恐怖片（horror movie），
　　　請根據圖片內容寫一篇約 50 字的簡短描述。

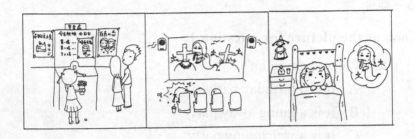

初級英檢模擬試題詳解③

一、聽力測驗

第一部份

Look at the picture for question 1.

1. (**A**) What is going on?
   A. It is a birthday party.
   B. It is a going away party.
   C. It is a welcoming party.

   * ***go on*** 發生 (= *happen*)　　***birthday party*** 慶生會
   going away party 歡送會　　***welcoming party*** 歡迎會

Look at the picture for question 2.

2. (**A**) How many people are swimming?
   A. Two.
   B. Four.
   C. Six.

   * swim〔swɪm〕*v.* 游泳

Look at the picture for question 3.

3. (**C**) What is Jimmy's favorite animal?
   A. Dog.
   B. Cat.
   C. Rabbit.

   * favorite〔'fevərɪt〕*adj.* 最喜愛的
   animal〔'ænəml̩〕*n.* 動物　　rabbit〔'ræbɪt〕*n.* 兔子

Look at the picture for question 4.

4. (**B**) What are they doing?

     A. They are playing ball.

     B. They are playing tennis.

     C. They are playing table tennis.

     * tennis〔'tɛnɪs〕*n.* 網球

       table tennis 桌球

Look at the picture for question 5.

5. (**B**) What happened to Barbara?

     A. She is resting.

     B. She is sick.

     C. She is sleeping.

     * rest〔rɛst〕*v.* 休息

       sick〔sɪk〕*adj.* 生病的

Look at the picture for question 6.

6. (**A**) How many people are fishing?

     A. One.

     B. Three.

     C. Five.

     * fish〔fɪʃ〕*v.* 釣魚

Look at the picture for question 7.

7. (**C**) What is the weather like?

    A. It is sunny and hot.

    B. It is wet and cold.

    C. It is sunny and breezy.

    * ***What is the weather like?*** 現在天氣怎麼樣？

    sunny〔'sʌnɪ〕*adj.* 陽光普照的　　wet〔wɛt〕*adj.* 潮濕的

    breezy〔'brizɪ〕*adj.* 有微風的

Look at the picture for question 8.

8. (**A**) How much is the hot dog?

    A. $1.50.

    B. $1.25.

    C. $1.75.

    * ***hot dog*** 熱狗

Look at the picture for question 9.

9. (**B**) What are they going to do?

    A. They are going to take a train.

    B. They are going to take a bus.

    C. They are going to take a plane.

    * take〔tek〕*v.* 搭乘

    plane〔plen〕*n.* 飛機（= *airplane*）

Look at the picture for question 10.

10. (**C**) Which description matches the picture?

    A. The cup is behind the radio.

    B. The radio is between the clock and the cup.

    C. The clock is in front of the radio.

    * description〔dɪˈskrɪpʃən〕 *n.* 敘述

      match〔mætʃ〕 *v.* 符合　　cup〔kʌp〕 *n.* 杯子

      bchind〔bɪˈhaɪnd〕 *prep.* 在～之後

      radio〔ˈredɪ,o〕 *n.* 收音機

      between〔bəˈtwin〕 *prep.* 在～之間

      in front of 在～的前面

第二部份

11. (**A**) What's for lunch?

    A. Chicken and rice.

    B. It's at 12:00.

    C. Thanks, but I'm not hungry.

    * lunch〔lʌntʃ〕 *n.* 午餐　　chicken〔ˈtʃɪkən〕 *n.* 雞肉

      rice〔raɪs〕 *n.* 米飯　　hungry〔ˈhʌŋgrɪ〕 *adj.* 飢餓的

12. (**C**) When did you see Jim?

    A. I will see him tomorrow.

    B. I see him every day.

    C. I saw him this morning.

    * tomorrow〔təˈmɔro〕 *n.* 明天

      this morning 今天早上

13. (**B**) Don't forget to take your umbrella.

A. I haven't.

B. I won't.

C. I didn't.

* forget〔fəˈgɛt〕v. 忘記

umbrella〔ʌmˈbrɛlə〕n. 雨傘

14. (**B**) What did you think of the movie?

A. I think I saw it last week.

B. It was wonderful!

C. I saw it with my brother.

* ***think of*** 認為　wonderful〔ˈwʌndəfəl〕adj. 很棒的

15. (**A**) Do you like to swim?

A. Yes, I like it very much.

B. Yes, you do.

C. Yes, it's a good day to go swimming.

* good〔gʊd〕adj. 適合的

16. (**B**) Have you finished the science report yet?

A. I reported it yesterday.

B. No, I haven't.

C. Yes, I do.

* finish〔ˈfɪnɪʃ〕v. 完成

science〔ˈsaɪəns〕n. 自然科學

report〔rɪˈport〕n. v. 報告　yet〔jɛt〕adv. 已經

17. (**A**) It looks like rain.

    A. Yes, it does.

    B. Yes, it is.

    C. No, it's not.

    * ***It looks like rain***. 看起來要下雨了。

18. (**A**) How long have you been waiting to see the doctor?

    A. Since twelve o'clock.

    B. You have to stand in line.

    C. I can't wait to see the doctor.

    * ***How long ~ ?*** ~多久？   wait〔wet〕*v.* 等待

    since〔sɪns〕*prep.* 自從   ***stand in line*** 排隊

    can't wait + to V. 等不及要~

19. (**B**) Do you like pets?

    A. Yes, I like to pet the dog.

    B. Yes, and I have a dog.

    C. I like dogs more than cats.

    * pet〔pɛt〕*n.* 寵物 *v.* 愛撫

20. (**B**) Oh! The floor is slippery.

    A. Yes, isn't it beautiful?

    B. Be careful.

    C. I slipped it this morning.

    * floor〔flor〕*n.* 地板   slippery〔'slɪpərɪ〕*adj.* 滑的

    Be careful. 小心。   slip〔slɪp〕*v.* 掙脫

第三部份

21. (**C**) W：I can't get this VCR to work. Can you help me?

M：I can try. What seems to be the problem?

W：I can't insert the cassette.

M：That's because there's no power. You have to plug it in first!

Question：Why can't the woman insert the video cassette?

A. The VCR is broken.

B. She has to plug the cassette in, not insert it.

C. The VCR has no power.

* **get** + **sth.** + **to V.** 使某物能夠~

VCR 卡式錄放影機 (= **video cassette recorder**)

work〔wɜk〕v. (機器)運轉   seem〔sim〕v. 似乎

problem〔'prɑbləm〕n. 問題   insert〔ɪn'sɝt〕v. 插入

cassette〔kæ'sɛt〕n. 錄影帶   power〔'pauɚ〕n. 電力

plug in 插上插頭   broken〔'brokən〕adj. 故障的

22. (**A**) M：Look! Somebody left a wallet on the bench.

W：We can send it back to the owner. Is his name inside?

M：No, but there is some money inside.

W：We'd better turn it in to the police then.

Question : What will the man and the woman do
with the wallet?

A. They will give it to a police officer.

B. They will send it back to the owner.

C. They will sell the wallet and send the money to
the owner.

* leave〔liv〕*v.* 遺留　　wallet〔'walɪt〕*n.* 皮夾
bench〔bɛntʃ〕*n.* 長椅　　***send back*** 送回
owner〔'onɚ〕*n.* 擁有者　　inside〔'ɪn'saɪd〕*adv.* 在裡面
had better + *V.* 最好　　***turn in*** 繳交 (= *hand in*)
the police 警方　　then〔ðɛn〕*adv.* 那麼
do with 處理　　***police officer*** 警察　　sell〔sɛl〕*v.* 賣

23.(**B**) M : Excuse me, can you tell me when the next show
starts?

W : The next show is at 12:30, but I'm afraid it's
sold out.

M : How about the one after that?

W : It starts at 2:15 and I have six seats left.

M : We'll take two.

Question : Why won't the man go to the 12:30 show?

A. He is afraid to go by himself.

B. There are no tickets left.

C. There are only two seats left, and he needs six.

* show〔ʃo〕*n.* 表演　　start〔stɑrt〕*v.* 開始
I'm afraid (that) ~　恐怕~　　***sell out*** 賣光
How about ~ ?　~如何？　　seat〔sit〕*n.* 座位
left〔lɛft〕*adj.* 剩下的　　take〔tek〕*v.* 買
be afraid + ***to V.*** 害怕　　***by oneself*** 獨自 (= *alone*)

24. (**A**) W：How did you do on Professor Brown's test this
　　　　　　　morning?

　　　　　M：Not bad.　Geography is not a difficult subject for me.

　　　　　W：Me, either.　How about yesterday's math test?

　　　　　M：Oh, that's my worst subject.　I did terribly on
　　　　　　　that test.

　　　　　Question：What is true about the man?

　　　　　A. He is better at geography than math.

　　　　　B. He failed the geography test because that is a
　　　　　　　difficult subject for him.

　　　　　C. He wishes that Professor Brown taught math.

　　* ***How did you do on the test?*** 你考試考得如何？
　　　professor〔prəˈfɛsə〕n. 教授
　　　geography〔dʒiˈɑgrəfɪ〕n. 地理
　　　difficult〔ˈdɪfəˌkʌlt〕adj. 困難的
　　　subject〔ˈsʌbdʒɪkt〕n. 科目　　math〔mæθ〕n. 數學
　　　worst〔wɜst〕adj. 最差的（bad 的最高級）
　　　terribly〔ˈtɛrəblɪ〕adv. 糟糕地　　***do terribly*** 考得很差
　　　true〔tru〕adj. 眞實的；正確的　　***be good at*** 擅長於
　　　fail〔fel〕v.（考試）不及格　　wish〔wɪʃ〕v. 希望

25. (**C**) M：Have you seen the paper today?

　　　　　W：No, I haven't.　What's new?

　　　　　M：There is a big storm coming.　It will start to rain
　　　　　　　tonight.

　　　　　W：Oh, no!　Not another typhoon!

Question: What does the man tell the woman?

A. He saw a big typhoon today.

B. The newspaper hasn't come yet.

C. A typhoon is coming.

* paper (ˋpepɚ) *n.* 報紙 (= *newspaper*)

What's new? 有什麼消息嗎?

storm (stɔrm) *n.* 暴風雨　　typhoon (taɪˋfun) *n.* 颱風

26. (**B**) M: Can you help me? I'm looking for the post office.

W: Sure. It's around the corner. But why do you want to go there?

M: I want to send this box to my brother.

Question: What does the man want the woman to do?

A. Help him carry the box.

B. Tell him where the post office is.

C. Give the box to his brother.

* *post office* 郵局　　*around the corner* 在轉角

send (sɛnd) *v.* 寄;送　　carry (ˋkærɪ) *v.* 搬運

27. (**A**) M: Excuse me, where can I find the ice cream?

W: Ice cream is in Aisle 12, with the frozen food.

M: Thank you.

Question: What does the man want?

A. He wants to buy some ice cream.

B. He wants to know where Aisle 12 is.

C. He wants to freeze some food.

* *ice cream* 冰淇淋　　aisle (aɪl) *n.* 通道;走道

frozen (ˋfrozn̩) *adj.* 冷凍的　　freeze (friz) *v.* 冷凍

28. (**C**) W：Can I help you, sir?

M：Fill it up, please, and clean the windshield, too.

W：Right away.

Question：Where does this conversation take place?

A. In front of a window.

B. In a restaurant.

C. At a gas station.

* ***fill up*** 使裝滿　***Fill it up.*** 把油加滿。

clean〔klin〕v. 清潔

windshield〔'wɪnd,ʃild〕n. 擋風玻璃　***right away*** 立刻

conversation〔,kɑnvɚ'seʃən〕n. 對話　***take place*** 發生

restaurant〔'rɛstərənt〕n. 餐廳　***gas station*** 加油站

29. (**C**) W：Which class is your favorite?

M：I like all of my classes except for math.

W：Why is that?

M：No matter how hard I study, I just can't do well on it.

Question：What does the man mean?

A. He likes all of his classes.

B. He doesn't like any of his classes.

C. Math is his least favorite class.

* favorite〔'fevərɪt〕n. 最喜愛的人或事物

except for 除～之外　***no matter*** 無論

hard〔hɑrd〕adv. 努力地　***do well*** 表現出色

mean〔min〕v. 意思是　　least〔list〕adv. 最不

30. (**B**) M：I'd like a number one meal, please.

W：I'm sorry, but you'll have to wait two minutes for the hamburger.

M：That's OK. Can I have my Coke while I wait?

W：No problem.

Question：What will the woman do next?

A. Give the man a hamburger.

B. Give the man a Coke.

C. Order a number two meal instead.

* ***would like*** 想要（= *want*）　　meal〔mil〕*n.*（一）餐
minute〔'mɪnɪt〕*n.* 分鐘
hamburger〔'hæmbɝgɚ〕*n.* 漢堡　　***That's OK.*** 沒關係。
Coke〔kok〕*n.* 可口可樂（= *Coca-cola*）
while〔hwaɪl〕*conj.* 當…的時候　　***No problem.*** 沒問題。
next〔nɛkst〕*adv.* 接下來　　order〔'ɔrdɚ〕*v.* 點餐
instead〔ɪn'stɛd〕*adv.* 作爲代替

二、閱讀能力測驗

第一部份：詞彙和結構

1. (**A**) Maggie closed her eyes and made a <u>wish</u>.

梅姬閉上眼睛，然後許了一個願望。

(A) ***wish***〔wɪʃ〕*n.* 願望　　***make a wish*** 許願

(B) cake〔kek〕*n.* 蛋糕　　make a cake 製作蛋糕

(C) tea〔ti〕*n.* 茶　　make tea 泡茶

(D) coffee〔'kɔfɪ〕*n.* 咖啡　　make coffee 泡咖啡

* close〔kloz〕*v.* 閉上　　glasses〔'glæsɪz〕*n. pl.* 眼鏡

2. (**C**) I'm sorry for breaking your glasses. It's all my <u>fault</u>.
　　　　我很抱歉把你的眼鏡打破了。這全都是我的<u>錯</u>。

　　　　(A) joke〔dʒok〕n. 笑話

　　　　(B) question〔'kwɛstʃən〕n. 問題

　　　　(C) ***fault***〔fɔlt〕n. 過錯

　　　　(D) idea〔aɪ'diə〕n. 主意；想法

　　　　* break〔brek〕v. 打破　　glasses〔'glæsɪz〕n. pl. 眼鏡

3. (**C**) Linda is very <u>brown</u> after her holiday in Thailand,
　　　　because the sun there is very hot.
　　　　琳達去泰國度假後，<u>皮膚曬得很黑</u>，因為那裡的太陽非常大。

　　　　(A) yellow〔'jɛlo〕adj. 黃色的

　　　　(B) black〔blæk〕adj. 黑色的

　　　　(C) ***brown***〔braʊn〕adj.（皮膚）曬黑的

　　　　(D) orange〔'ɔrɪndʒ〕adj. 橙色的

　　　　* holiday〔'hɑlə,de〕n. 假期　　Thailand〔'taɪlənd〕n. 泰國
　　　　sun〔sʌn〕n. 太陽；陽光

4. (**A**) I feel it is great to take <u>a bath</u> in the hot springs in
　　　　Yangmingshan. 我覺得在陽明山<u>泡溫泉</u>很棒。

　　　　(A) ***take a bath*** 泡澡

　　　　　　take a bath in the hot springs 泡溫泉

　　　　(B) take a trip 去旅行 < *to* >

　　　　(C) take medicine 吃藥

　　　　(D) take an interest in 對…有興趣

　　　　* great〔gret〕adj. 很棒的

5. (**B**) Paul : I'm going to the Taipei City Hall. Bus Number
286 goes there, <u>doesn't it</u>?

Rita : Yes, but you can take the MRT, too.

保羅：我要去台北市政府。286 號公車有到那裡，<u>不是嗎</u>？

莉塔：沒錯，但是你也可以搭捷運。

前面是肯定句，附加問句必須是否定句，且 goes 是一般
動詞，故助動詞用 does，代名詞則用 it 代替 bus number
286，選 (B) **doesn't it**，就是 doesn't it go there 的省略
疑問句。

* **city hall** 市政府
MRT 捷運 (= *Mass Rapid Transit*)

6. (**B**) George was <u>showing off</u> his new bicycle to his
classmates this morning, but he found that his bicycle
had been stolen after school.

喬治今天早上向他的同學<u>炫耀</u>他的新腳踏車，但是在放學
後，他發現他的腳踏車被偷了。

(A) take off 脫掉

(B) **show off** 炫耀

(C) wait for 等待

(D) laugh at 取笑

* classmate〔'klæs,met〕*n.* 同學
steal〔stil〕*v.* 偷（三態變化為：steal-stole-stolen）
after school 放學後

7. (**B**) Mike and I <u>spent</u> all night decorating our new house.
麥克跟我<u>花</u>了整晚的時間佈置我們的新房子。

> 「花費時間」的表達方式有：
>
> $\begin{cases} 人 + \textbf{\textit{spend}} + 時間 + (\textbf{\textit{in}}) + \textbf{\textit{V-ing}} \\ 事或 It + \textbf{\textit{take}} + (人) + 時間 + \textbf{\textit{to V.}} \end{cases}$
>
> 而 (C) cost「（東西）值（多少錢）」，(D) pay「付費」，
> 用法皆不合。

* decorate〔ˈdɛkəˌret〕v. 佈置

8. (**B**) Tim is an active language learner. He always carries a
<u>dictionary</u> with him.
提姆是個主動的語言學習者。他總是隨身攜帶一本<u>字典</u>。

(A) story〔ˈstorɪ〕n. 故事
(B) **dictionary**〔ˈdɪkʃənˌɛrɪ〕n. 字典
(C) conversation〔ˌkɑnvɚˈseʃən〕n. 對話
(D) sentence〔ˈsɛntəns〕n. 句子

* active〔ˈæktɪv〕adj. 主動的
 language〔ˈlæŋgwɪdʒ〕n. 語言　　carry〔ˈkærɪ〕v. 攜帶

9. (**A**) Stop <u>singing</u>! What a terrible voice you have!
停止唱歌！你的歌聲真糟糕！

> stop 的用法：
>
> $\begin{cases} \text{stop} + \text{V-ing} \quad 停止做（一個動作） \\ \text{stop} + \text{to V.} \quad 停下來，去做（二個動作） \end{cases}$

* terrible〔ˈtɛrəbl̩〕adj. 糟糕的
 voice〔vɔɪs〕n. 聲音

10. (**D**) Melissa : Mom, I got the best grade on the English
　　　　　　test today.
　　　　Mother : Good job, daughter.　I'm <u>proud</u> of you.
　　　　梅麗莎：媽媽，我今天英文考試考最高分。
　　　　媽　媽：做得好，女兒。我<u>以妳為榮</u>。

　　　　(A) sick〔sɪk〕*adj.* 生病的
　　　　(B) tired〔taɪrd〕*adj.* 疲倦的
　　　　(C) sure〔ʃʊr〕*adj.* 確信的
　　　　(D) ***proud***〔praʊd〕*adj.* 光榮的 < *of* >
　　　　　　be proud of 以～為榮

　　　* grade〔gred〕*n.* 分數；成績　　test〔tɛst〕*n.* 考試
　　　good job 做得好　　daughter〔'dɔtɚ〕*n.* 女兒

11. (**D**) Nancy <u>was selling</u> fake CDs when the police came.
　　　　警察來時，南茜<u>正在賣</u>仿冒的 CD。

　　　　按照句意為過去的時間，故選 (D) ***was selling***，「過去
　　　　進行式」表「過去某段時間正在進行的動作」。

　　　* fake〔fek〕*adj.* 仿冒的　　***the police*** 警方

12. (**B**) With e-mails and telephones, <u>communication</u> has become
　　　　easier, and the world is getting smaller.
　　　　有了電子郵件和電話，<u>通訊</u>已變得更容易，世界變得越來越小。

　　　　(A) difference〔'dɪfrəns〕*n.* 差別
　　　　(B) ***communication***〔kə,mjunə'keʃən〕*n.* 通訊
　　　　(C) software〔'sɔft,wɛr〕*n.* 軟體
　　　　(D) housework〔'haʊs,wɝk〕*n.* 家事

　　　* e-mail〔'i,mel〕*n.* 電子郵件　　world〔wɝld〕*n.* 世界

13. (**C**) Fred and Jack are good friends, and <u>both of them</u> are basketball fans.

弗瑞德和傑克是好朋友,而且他們<u>兩人都</u>是籃球迷。

弗瑞德和傑克共兩個人,故代名詞用 both「兩者都」。
(A) all 指「(三者以上的)全部」,(B) one of them 須接單數動詞,(D) some of them「他們當中有一些人」,用法皆不合。

* fan〔fæn〕n. 迷

14. (**C**) My father came into the kitchen to see what was <u>wrong</u>.

我爸爸走進廚房,看看有什麼<u>不對勁</u>。

(A) bad〔bæd〕adj. 壞的
(B) right〔raɪt〕adj. 正確的
(C) **wrong**〔wɔŋ〕adj. 不對勁的
(D) long〔lɔŋ〕adj. 長的

15. (**D**) (In the teachers' office)

Miss Ho : Mr. Ma, <u>are there</u> students in the classroom?

Mr. Ma : I don't think so. School is over.

Miss Ho : But I hear people talking over there.

(在老師辦公室內)

何老師:馬老師,教室裡<u>有</u>學生嗎?

馬老師:我想沒有學生了。已經下課了。

何老師:可是我聽到有人在那裡講話。

「there + be 動詞」表「有」,又 students 為複數名詞,故 be 動詞用複數動詞 are。

* office〔'ɔfɪs〕n. 辦公室   school〔skul〕n. 上課
over〔'ovæ〕adj. 結束的   **over there** 在那裡

第二部份：段落填空

Questions 16-20

　　Learning English <u>is</u> an interesting thing. It's just <u>like</u> playing
　　　　　　　　　16　　　　　　　　　　　　　　　　　17
basketball. First, we have to memorize new words. If we don't
understand <u>them</u>, we have to <u>look them up</u> in the dictionary. And
　　　　　　　18　　　　　　　　　19
then we have to practice <u>as often as</u> we can. If we don't miss any
　　　　　　　　　　　　　20
chance to do these things, our English will get better and better.

　　學習英文是件有趣的事。就好像打籃球一樣。首先，我們必須背新
的單字。如果不懂的話，就必須查字典。然後必須儘可能地多加練習。
如果我們不放過任何學英文的機會，我們的英文就會變得愈來愈好。

　　　　interesting〔'ɪntrɪstɪŋ〕*adj.* 有趣的
　　　　memorize〔'mɛmə,raɪz〕*v.* 記憶；背誦
　　　　understand〔,ʌndɚ'stænd〕*v.* 了解
　　　　practice〔'præktɪs〕*v.* 練習　　miss〔mɪs〕*v.* 錯過
　　　　chance〔tʃæns〕*n.* 機會

16. (**D**)　動名詞當主詞，須視爲單數，且按照句意，學習英文「是」
　　　　　　件有趣的事，故選 (D) *is*。

17. (**B**)　依句意，選介系詞 (B) *like*「像」。而 (A) as「正如」，用於
　　　　　　「as…as～」，表「像～一樣…」，在此用法不合；(C) same
　　　　　　〔sem〕*adj.* 相同的，則不合句意。

18. (**C**)　代名詞 *them* 代替前面提到的名詞 new words。

19. (**D**) ⎧ ***look at*** 看（不可分片語）
　　　　　 ⎩ ***look up*** 查閱（可分片語）

　　　可分片語接受詞時，若受詞為代名詞，必須置於動詞及
　　　介系詞中間。

20. (**A**) ***as…as one can*** 表「儘可能…」（= *as…as possible*），依句
　　　意，選 (A) ***practice as often as possible***「儘可能經常練習」。
　　　而 (B) as well as「以及；和～一樣好」，(C) seldom〔ˈsɛldəm〕
　　　adv. 很少，均不合句意。

Questions 21-25

　　In the south of Taiwan, there is a very special place. <u>It has
clean beaches,</u> great weather, and beautiful forests. That place
　　　　21
is Kenting National Park. Every year, millions of people <u>visit the
park.</u> They come from all over Taiwan. People go there on　　22
honeymoons, school trips, and short weekend <u>holidays.</u> Also,
　　　　　　　　　　　　　　　　　　　　　　　　　　23
tourists from other countries love to visit the park.

　　台灣南部有一個非常特別的地方。那裡有乾淨的海灘、很棒的天氣，
以及美麗的森林。那地方就是墾丁國家公園。每年有數百萬的人會到這
公園遊覽。他們來自台灣各地。人們去那裡度蜜月、校外教學，以及度
過短期的週末假日。此外，其他國家的觀光客也喜歡來這個公園遊覽。

　　　　south〔saυθ〕*n.* 南部　　special〔ˈspɛʃəl〕*adj.* 特別的
　　　　forest〔ˈfɔrɪst〕*n.* 森林　　***national park*** 國家公園
　　　　millions of 數百萬計的　　***all over*** 遍及
　　　　honeymoon〔ˈhʌnɪˌmun〕*n.* 蜜月旅行
　　　　tourist〔ˈtυrɪst〕*n.* 觀光客

At Kenting, <u>there is a lot to do</u>. You can play in the water
24

and relax on the beach. You can also visit the beautiful gardens

and <u>look at</u> the strange rocks with funny shapes. They have names
25

like "frog rock" and "sail rock."

在墾丁有很多東西可以玩。你可以玩水，在海灘放鬆一下。也可以
參觀那些美麗的花園，並且看看那些奇形怪狀的石頭。這些石頭有名字
的，如「青蛙石」及「帆船石」。

relax〔rɪ'læks〕v. 放鬆　　beach〔bitʃ〕n. 海灘
garden〔'gardn̩〕n. 花園　　rock〔rɑk〕n. 岩石
funny〔'fʌnɪ〕adj. 奇特的　　shape〔ʃep〕n. 形狀
frog〔frɑg〕n. 青蛙　　sail〔sel〕n. 帆；帆船

21. (**C**) (A) 它並不貴
　　　　(B) 人們都很友善　　friendly〔'frɛndlɪ〕adj. 友善的
　　　　(C) 它有乾淨的海灘，
　　　　(D) 你可以看到雪，　　snow〔sno〕n. 雪

22. (**A**) (A) 遊覽這座公園　　(B) 擔心海灘
　　　　(C) 去台北　　　　　　(D) 留在家裡

23. (**C**) *weekend holidays* 週末假期

24. (**B**) (A) 很無聊　　　　　(B) 有很多事情可做
　　　　(C) 你會玩得不愉快　　(D) 沒什麼事情可做

25. (**B**) 依句意，「看」石頭，選 (B) *look at*。

第三部份：閱讀理解

Questions 26-27

Joseph and Nina are walking in a park.

Nina　：You threw your garbage on the ground. Pick it up.

Joseph：Why? It's only a small bag. Anyway, it's empty.

Nina　：We have to keep the park clean.

Joseph：But a lot of people do <u>the same thing</u>.

Nina　：I know. Those people are wrong.

約瑟夫與妮娜正在公園散步。

妮　娜：你怎麼把垃圾丟在地上。快撿起來。

約瑟夫：為什麼？就一個小袋子而已。反正，它是空的。

妮　娜：我們要保持公園的整潔。

約瑟夫：可是有很多人都做<u>一樣</u>的事啊。

妮　娜：我知道。那些人都做錯了。

> throw〔θro〕v. 丟棄（三態變化為：throw-threw-thrown）
> garbage〔'gɑrbɪdʒ〕n. 垃圾　　ground〔graʊnd〕n. 地面
> **pick up** 撿起　　anyway〔'ɛnɪ,we〕adv. 反正；無論如何
> empty〔'ɛmptɪ〕adj. 空的　　keep〔kip〕v. 保持
> clean〔klin〕adj. 乾淨的　　wrong〔rɔŋ〕adj. 錯誤的

26. (**B**) 妮娜

　　　(A) 把東西丟在地上。　　　(B) <u>很關心公園。</u>

　　　(C) 同意約瑟夫的說法。　　(D) 做錯事。

　　　* *care about* 關心
　　　　agree with sb. 同意某人的說法

27. (**D**) "the same thing" 指的是什麼？

    (A) 在公園散步。   (B) 撿起他們的垃圾。

    (C) 保持公園整潔。   (D) <u>把垃圾丟在地上。</u>

Questions 28-30

    Many people have the wrong idea about pigs. In fact, pigs are very clean animals. On farms, they live in dirty places, so they become very dirty. <u>In the wild</u>, pigs keep very clean.

    很多人都對豬有誤解。事實上，豬是非常乾淨的動物。在農場裡，他們住在髒亂的地方，所以也變得很髒。<u>在野外</u>，豬是非常愛乾淨的。

> ***in fact*** 事實上   **dirty** [ˈdɝtɪ] *adj.* 骯髒的
> **wild** [waɪld] *n.* 野生   ***in the wild*** 在野外

    They are also really smart. They may be smarter than dogs. So, pigs can learn things from people. Pigs are very friendly animals. Some people raise them as pets. Of course, people raise the small kind, not the big kind. Small pigs are very cute and they don't break things in the house. Big pigs usually live outside on farms, not in people's houses.

    牠們真的也很聰明。也許比狗還聰明。所以，豬也可以向人學東西。豬是非常友善的動物。有些人把牠們當寵物養。當然，人類養的是小型而不是大型的豬。小豬是很可愛的。而且牠們不會打破家裡的東西。大型豬通常都養在戶外的農場，而不會住在人的家裡。

> **smart** [smɑrt] *adj.* 聰明的   **friendly** [ˈfrɛndlɪ] *adj.* 友善的
> **raise** [rez] *v.* 飼養   **pet** [pɛt] *n.* 寵物
> **kind** [kaɪnd] *n.* 種類   **cute** [kjut] *adj.* 可愛的
> **break** [brek] *v.* 打破   **outside** [ˈaʊtˈsaɪd] *adv.* 在戶外

28. (**D**) 豬是 ＿＿＿＿＿＿＿＿＿＿ 。

　　(A) 又髒又笨的

　　(B) 害羞而且奇怪的

　　(C) 既危險又不友善的

　　(D) 聰明又溫和的

　　* stupid〔'stjupɪd〕*adj.* 愚蠢的　　shy〔ʃaɪ〕*adj.* 害羞的
　　　strange〔strendʒ〕*adj.* 奇怪的
　　　dangerous〔'dendʒərəs〕*adj.* 危險的
　　　unfriendly〔ʌn'frɛndlɪ〕*adj.* 不友善的（↔ *friendly*）
　　　gentle〔'dʒɛntḷ〕*adj.* 溫和的

29. (**A**) 第三行裡的 "in the wild" 是什麼意思？

　　(A) 在大自然裡。

　　(B) 在農場。

　　(C) 發瘋。

　　(D) 在人的家裡。

　　* line〔laɪn〕*n.* 行　　nature〔'netʃɚ〕*n.* 大自然
　　　crazy〔'krezɪ〕*adj.* 瘋狂的

30. (**D**) 下列何者為真？

　　(A) 豬喜歡髒兮兮的。

　　(B) 只有農民養豬。

　　(C) 狗比豬聰明。

　　(D) 有人在家中飼養小型的豬。

　　* following〔'faləwɪŋ〕*adj.* 下列的
　　　true〔tru〕*adj.* 真實的；正確的
　　　dirty〔'dɝtɪ〕*adj.* 髒的

Questions 31-32

這是一張電視節目表。閱讀後，回答問題。

時間	節目
7:00	氣象報告
7:30	快樂英語
8:00	世界新聞
9:00	流行時尚

schedule〔'skɛdʒul〕n. 時間表
program〔'progræm〕n. 節目　　report〔rɪ'port〕n. 報導
news〔njuz〕n. 新聞　　fashion〔'fæʃən〕n. 流行

31. (**A**) 莎拉明天想和朋友去海邊玩。她應該在什麼時候看電視，
　　　知道會不會下雨？

　　　想知道是否會下雨，要看「氣象報告」，故選 (A) 7:00。

32. (**C**) 彼得想知道全世界發生了什麼事情，所以他應該在幾點鐘
　　　打開電視？

　　　想知道全球時事，要看「世界新聞」，故選 (C) 8:00。

　　* happen〔'hæpən〕v. 發生
　　　around the world 在全世界
　　　turn on 打開（電器）

Questions 33-35

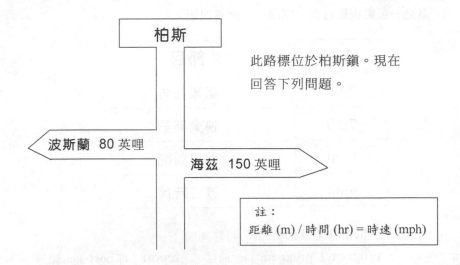

此路標位於柏斯鎮。現在
回答下列問題。

註：
距離 (m) / 時間 (hr) = 時速 (mph)

sign〔saɪn〕*n.* 標誌　　*road sign* 路標
stand〔stænd〕*v.* 位於　　mile〔maɪl〕*n.* 英哩
mph 每小時英哩數；時數（= *miles per hour*）

33. (**C**) 蘿拉要從柏斯開車前往波特蘭。她以每小時四十英哩的速度
行駛。她在下午兩點鐘從柏斯出發。她何時會到達波特蘭？

根據公式，假設蘿拉從柏斯開車到波特蘭，要花 X 小時，
即 80 (m) / X = 40 (mph)，故 X = 2 (hr)，她於下午兩
點鐘出發，加上兩個小時的車程，所以到達波特蘭的時間
是下午四點鐘。

* leave〔liv〕*v.* 離開　　*get to* 到達

34. (**D**) 賈士柏要從柏斯開車前往海茲。他以每小時五十英哩的速度行駛。他將在途中停留兩個小時看表演。他在早上十點鐘從柏斯出發。他何時會到達海茲？

根據公式，假設賈士柏從柏斯開車到海茲，要花 X 小時，即 150 (m) / X = 50 (mph)，故 X = 3 (hr)，他於早上十點出發，加上兩個小時的看表演時間後，再加上三個小時的車程，到達海茲的時間是下午三點鐘。

* show〔ʃo〕*n.* 表演
on the way 在途中

35. (**B**) 琳達要去波特蘭，參加她朋友的派對。派對將在晚上七點鐘開始。她想提早三十分鐘到。如果她以每小時四十英哩的速度行駛，她應該何時離開柏斯？

根據公式，假設琳達從柏斯開車到波特蘭，要花 X 小時，即 80 (m) / X = 40 (mph)，故 X = 2 (hr)，她預定在晚上六點半到波特蘭，減去兩個小時的車程，即應在下午四點半，從柏斯出發。

三、寫作能力測驗

第一部份：單句寫作

第 1～5 題：句子改寫

1. Getting a lot of lucky money is a happy thing.
   It's _____.

   > 重點結構：以 It 為虛主詞引出的句子
   >
   > 解　答：It's a happy thing to get a lot of lucky money.
   >
   > 句型分析：It's + 名詞 + to V.
   >
   > 說　明：It 代替不定詞片語做主詞，不定詞片語則擺在句尾，
   > 　　　　故 getting a lot of lucky money 改為 to get a lot of
   > 　　　　lucky money。
   >
   > ＊ lucky〔ˈlʌkɪ〕adj. 幸運的　***lucky money*** 壓歲錢

2. I made my dog sit down.
   My dog _____ by me.

   > 重點結構：動詞 make 被動語態的用法
   >
   > 解　答：My dog was made to sit down by me.
   >
   > 句型分析：主詞 + be 動詞 + made + to V.
   >
   > 說　明：「make + 受詞 + 原形 V.」表「叫～做…」，若改為
   > 　　　　被動語態，原形動詞須改為不定詞。

3. I will never forget the good time we spent together.
   Never _____.

   > 重點結構：never 置於句首的用法
   >
   > 解　答：Never will I forget the good time we spent
   > 　　　　together.

句型分析：Never + 助動詞 + 主詞 + 原形動詞

　說　明：never 為否定副詞，置於句首加強語氣時，主詞與
　　　　　動詞須倒裝。

4.　It rains a lot in winter in Taipei.

　We _____.

　重點結構：rain 的用法

　　解　答：<u>We have a lot of rain in winter in Taipei.</u>

　句型分析：We + have + rain + 時間副詞 + 地方副詞

　　說　明：表「下雨」的說法有三種：

　　　　　　It *rains*.（rain 是動詞）

　　　　　　We have *rain*.（rain 是不可數名詞）

　　　　　　There is *rain*.（rain 是不可數名詞）

　　　　　a lot 是副詞片語，表「許多」，修飾動詞，若要修飾
　　　　　名詞，須改為 a lot of，表「許多的」。

5.　I spent two hours practicing playing soccer.

　It _____.

　重點結構：take 的用法

　　解　答：<u>It took me two hours to practice playing soccer.</u>

　句型分析：It takes + *sb*. + to V.

　　說　明：「花費時間」的用法：

　　　　　　人 + spend + 一段時間 + V-ing

　　　　　　事物或 It + take + 人 + 一段時間 + to V.

　　　　　spent 是過去式動詞，故 take 要改成過去式動詞

　　　　　took，practicing 要改成不定詞 to practice。

* soccer〔'sɑkɚ〕*n.* 足球

第 6～10 題：句子合併

6. Study hard. (用 and)
   You will get good grades.

   _____ .

       重點結構：祈使句表達條件句的用法
        解   答：Study hard, and you will get good grades.
       句型分析：祈使句, and + 主詞 + 動詞
        說   明：此句型表「如果…，就～」。本句可改為：
                     If you study hard, you will get good grades.

7. I want to know the girl. (用 with 合併)
   That girl has short hair.

   _____ .

       重點結構：with 的用法
        解   答：I want to know the girl with short hair.
       句型分析：I want to know the girl + with + 名詞
        說   明：介系詞 with 在此表「有」，相當於 having。
                     with short hair 用來修飾 the girl。

8. The coffee is very hot. (用 so…that 合併)
   I can't drink it.

   _____ .

       重點結構：so…that～ 的用法
        解   答：The coffee is so hot that I can't drink it.

句型分析：主詞 + be 動詞 + so + 形容詞 + that 子句

　說　明：這題的意思是說「咖啡太燙，所以我沒辦法喝」。用 so…that～ 合併兩句，表「如此…以致於～」。

9. I didn't see you yesterday. (用 either 合併)
   I didn't see you the day before yesterday.
   I didn't _____, and I didn't _____.

　重點結構：either 的用法
　　解　答：I didn't see you yesterday, and I didn't (see you) the day before yesterday(,) either.
　句型分析：主詞 + 動詞，and + 主詞 + 動詞 + (,) either.
　　說　明：否定句的「也」，用 either，擺在句尾，之前的逗號可寫，也可不寫。

　* *the day before yesterday*　前天

10. A man wants to see you. (用 who 合併)
    The man is called Dr. Wang.
    A man who _____.

　重點結構：由 who 引導的形容詞子句
　　解　答：A man who is called Dr. Wang wants to see you.
　句型分析：A man + who + 動詞 + 名詞 + 動詞
　　說　明：這題的意思是說「有位王醫生想要見你」，在合併時，用 who 代替先行詞 A man，引導形容詞子句。

　* call 〔kɔl〕v. 稱爲

第 11～15 題：重組

11. What _____?

    she / usually / does / do / Sundays / on

      重點結構：wh-問句的用法

       解　答：<u>What does she usually do on Sundays?</u>

      句型分析：What + 助動詞 + 主詞 + 動詞？

       説　明：What 引導的問句中，主詞為第三人稱單數，故助動
            詞用 does，而不是 do；頻率副詞 usually 置於助動
            詞 does 之後，一般動詞 do 之前。

    * **on Sundays** 每個星期天（ = *every Sunday*）

12. Would _____?

    kind / to give / a / enough / you / me / be / hand

      重點結構：enough 的用法

       解　答：<u>Would you be kind enough to give me a hand?</u>

      句型分析：be 動詞 + 形容詞 + enough + to V.

       説　明：這題的意思是說「你能不能好心點，幫我一個忙？」
            副詞 enough 須置於形容詞之後，後面再接不定詞
            片語，表「夠…，足以～」。

    * kind〔kaɪnd〕*adj.* 好心的
      give sb. a hand 幫助某人（ = *help sb.*）

13. I _____.

    to / frightened / too / open / my / am / eyes

      重點結構：「too + 形容詞 + to V.」的用法

       解　答：<u>I am too frightened to open my eyes.</u>

句型分析：主詞 + be 動詞 + too + 形容詞 + to V.

說　明：這題的意思是說「我太害怕了，不敢張開眼睛」，用 too…to V. 合併，表「太…以致於不～」。

* frightened〔'fraɪtn̩d〕adj.（人）害怕的

14. Our teacher ＿＿＿＿＿＿＿＿＿＿＿＿＿＿＿＿＿＿＿＿.

how / teaches / to / us / sing / songs / English

重點結構：teach 的用法

解　答：Our teacher teaches us how to sing English songs.

句型分析：主詞 + teach + 受詞 + 疑問詞 + to V.

說　明：teach 的用法為：

$$\begin{cases} teach + sb. + sth. \\ teach + sth. + to + sb. \end{cases}$$

所列出的單字中，to 是不定詞的 to，不是介系詞的 to，故用第一種方式重組。「疑問詞 + to V.」，構成「名詞片語」，做動詞 teaches 的受詞。

15. It ＿＿＿＿＿＿＿＿＿＿＿＿＿＿＿＿＿＿＿＿.

must / frightening / to / a ghost / be / see

重點結構：以 It 為虛主詞引出的句子

解　答：It must be frightening to see a ghost.

句型分析：It + 助動詞 + be 動詞 + 形容詞 + 不定詞

說　明：虛主詞 it 代替不定詞片語，不定詞片語 to see a ghost 則放在句尾，整句的意思是「看見鬼一定很可怕」。

* must〔mʌst〕aux. 一定　　frightening〔'fraɪtnɪŋ〕adj. 可怕的
ghost〔gost〕n. 鬼

第二部份：段落寫作

題目： 昨天妳/你和姐姐及她的男朋友去看恐怖片(horror movie)，
　　　 請根據圖片內容寫一篇約 50 字的簡短描述。

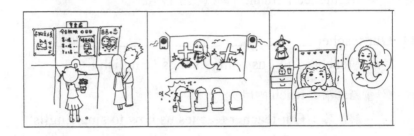

Yesterday was a holiday. I went to the movies with my sister and her boyfriend. I wanted to see the new cartoon movie and my sister wanted to see a love story, **but** her boyfriend wanted to see a horror movie. He bought the tickets, so we went to see the scary movie. I was scared to death in the movie. I covered my eyes and screamed. **Finally**, it was over.

When I went to bed, I couldn't forget the movie. I kept thinking about the ghost and stayed awake all night. **Next time** I go to the movies, I will not choose a horror movie.

> ***go to the movies*** 去看電影　　cartoon (kɑr'tun) *n.* 卡通
> ***horror movie*** 恐怖片 (– *scary movie*)
> scary ('skɛrɪ) *adj.* 可怕的　　scare (skɛr) *v.* 驚嚇
> ***be scared to death*** 嚇得要死；非常害怕
> cover ('kʌvə) *v.* 覆蓋　　scream (skrim) *v.* 尖叫
> finally ('faɪnḷɪ) *adv.* 最後；終於
> keep (kip) *v.* 持續　　stay (ste) *v.* 保持
> awake (ə'wek) *adj.* 清醒的　　choose (tʃuz) *v.* 選擇

全民英語能力分級檢定測驗

初級測驗④

一、聽力測驗

　　本測驗分三部份，全為三選一之選擇題，每部份各 10 題，共 30 題，作答時間約 20 分鐘。

第一部份：　看圖辨義

　　　　　　本部份共 10 題，試題冊上每題有一個圖片，請聽錄音機播出一個相關的問題，與 A、B、C 三個英語敘述後，選一個與所看到圖片最相符的答案，並在答案紙上相對的圓圈內塗黑作答。每題播出一遍，問題及選項均不印在試題冊上。

例：（看）

NT$80　　NT$50

（聽）

Look at the picture.　How much is the hamburger?

　　A.　It's eighty dollars.

　　B.　It's fifty-five dollars.

　　C.　It's eighteen dollars.

正確答案為 A

Question 1

Question 2

Question 3

Question 4

Question 5

Question 6

請 翻 頁 ⟹

Question 7

Question 8

Question 9

Question 10

請 翻 頁 ⬛⬛⬛⟹

第二部份：問答

本部份共 10 題，每題錄音機會播出一個問句或直述句，每題播出一次，聽後請從試題冊上 A、B、C 三個選項中，選出一個最適合的回答或回應，並在答案紙上塗黑作答。

例：

（聽） Good morning, Kevin. How are you?

（看） A. I'm fine, thank you.
　　　 B. I'm in the living room.
　　　 C. My name is Kevin.

正確答案為 A

11. A. I get up at six o'clock on school days.
　　B. About seven-thirty.
　　C. I take the bus to school.

12. A. They are all fine, thank you.
　　B. There are six, including me.
　　C. My brother is older than I.

13. A. I came here by bus.
　　B. I just came from the supermarket.
　　C. Hualien is my hometown.

14. A. I don't want to move to Taichung.
　　B. That was a good movie.
　　C. That's a good idea.

15. A. Here you are.
    B. Thank you.
    C. It cost $100.

16. A. It was a holiday.
    B. I went to the mountains.
    C. I don't go to school on Sundays.

17. A. I ran out of milk.
    B. It was a nice day.
    C. I wanted to borrow a book.

18. A. How about the park?
    B. Let's go before lunch.
    C. Let's go to McDonald's.

19. A. I hope I can remember all the dates.
    B. I think I did pretty well.
    C. I forgot some important formulas.

20. A. It was too expensive.
    B. I was sick.
    C. My boss gave me the day off.

請 翻 頁 ◀──▷

第三部份：　簡短對話

　　　　　本部份共 10 題，每題錄音機會播出一段對話及一個相關
　　　　　的問題，每題播出兩次，聽後請從試題冊上 A、B、C 三
　　　　　個選項中，選出一個最適合的回答，並在答案紙上塗黑
　　　　　作答。

　　　　　例：

　　（聽）(Woman)　Good afternoon, …Mr. Davis?

　　　　　(Man)　　Yes.　I have an appointment with
　　　　　　　　　 Dr. Sanders at two o'clock.　My
　　　　　　　　　 son Tommy has a fever.

　　　　　(Woman)　Oh, that's too bad.　Well, please
　　　　　　　　　 have a seat, Mr. Davis.　Dr.
　　　　　　　　　 Sanders will be right with you.

　　　　　Question:　Where did this conversation take
　　　　　　　　　　　place?

　　（看）A.　In a post office.
　　　　　B.　In a restaurant.
　　　　　C.　In a doctor's office.

　　　　　正確答案為 C

21. A.　On a plane.
　　 B.　In a taxi.
　　 C.　On the MRT.

22. A.　Go to Macy's today.
　　 B.　Close the store.
　　 C.　Pay for their purchases.

23. A. Spring.
    B. Summer.
    C. Winter.

24. A. She will call the
       bookstore.
    B. She will buy the
       Harry Potter books.
    C. She will visit Harry
       Potter.

25. A. She is afraid to go to
       the bus station.
    B. She doesn't know
       where the bus station
       is.
    C. She likes the new
       bus station.

26. A. He is drinking tea
       because he is cold.
    B. He is taking
       medicine.
    C. He is drinking a
       delicious cold drink.

27. A. She will take her
       grandmother to a movie.
    B. She will see a movie with
       her friends.
    C. She will keep her
       grandmother company.

28. A. They will eat their lunch
       outside in the mountains.
    B. They will go out for lunch
       at a fast-food restaurant.
    C. They will eat on the way
       to the mountains.

29. A. He put it on the table.
    B. He gave it to his mother.
    C. He moved it to a secret
       hiding-place.

30. A. He watched TV late at
       night.
    B. He fell asleep while
       watching TV.
    C. He told the woman what
       time it was.

請 翻 頁

二、閱讀能力測驗

本測驗分三部份，全爲四選一之選擇題，共 35 題，作答時間 35 分鐘。

第一部份：詞彙和結構

本部份共 15 題，每題含一個空格。請就試題冊上 A、B、C、D 四個選項中選出最適合題意的字或詞，標示在答案紙上。

1. Can I borrow your _____ to make a call?
   A. dining room
   B. air conditioner
   C. cell phone
   D. soft drink

2. Whenever we sing in the KTV parlor, Sally always holds the microphone. I think she likes to _____.
   A. stay up
   B. get up
   C. give up
   D. show off

3. After eating the pizza, we asked the waiter for more _____ to wipe our oily hands.
   A. menus
   B. forks
   C. glasses
   D. napkins

4. Linda put on ten kilograms during the summer vacation, so she decided to go _____ a diet.
   A. on
   B. up
   C. with
   D. in

5. George and Karen are afraid of their mother, because she is _____ with them.
   A. kind
   B. nice
   C. worried
   D. strict

6. The "thinking" car can slow down by itself if it is too _____ to the car in front.
   A. quick
   B. close
   C. fast
   D. direct

7. The book was _____ that the girl found it hard to put it down.
   A. so interested
   B. too interested
   C. so interesting
   D. too interested

請 翻 頁 ⬛⟹

8. Working overseas often _____ that you have to speak a foreign language.

   A. mean

   B. means

   C. is to mean

   D. meaning

9. Bruce is an American and has been in Taiwan for more than ten years. He can speak not _____ Chinese but also Taiwanese.

   A. very

   B. that

   C. only

   D. less

10. Sandy and Sally are twins, but they are not like _____.

    A. each other

    B. the other

    C. another

    D. both

11. Please sit down and _____ the instructions carefully.

    A. reads

    B. read

    C. to read

    D. reading

12. My hair is darker than _____.

A. them

B. your

C. ours

D. hers

13. What a wonderful winter vacation! We don't have _____ homework.

A. many

B. much

C. little

D. some

14. Miss Li works in a fast-food restaurant in Taipei. She _____ there since she graduated from senior high school.

A. was

B. is

C. has been

D. will be

15. _____ you see her, give her this important letter.

A. If

B. Because

C. So

D. Although

請 翻 頁 ◀▢══▷

第二部份：段落填空

　　　　本部份共 10 題，包括二個段落，每個段落各含 5 個空格。
　　　　請就試題冊上 A、B、C、D 四個選項中選出最適合題意
　　　　的字或詞，標示在答案紙上。

Questions 16-20

　　We need our eyes to do a lot of things.　Remember
___(16)___ enough light when you study at the desk.　If you
can't see ___(17)___, you should go to the eye doctor to have
your eyes ___(18)___.　The doctor will write a ___(19)___ for
you.　Take it to a store and buy ___(20)___.

16. A. use
　　B. to use
　　C. using
　　D. to be used

17. A. fast
　　B. clear
　　C. strong
　　D. well

18. A. cleaned
　　B. celebrated
　　C. changed
　　D. examined

19. A. letter
　　B. sentence
　　C. prescription
　　D. e-mail

20. A. a good pair of glasses
　　B. a glass
　　C. a piece of glasses
　　D. a pair of fashionable
　　　　glass

Questions 21-25

Dear Mom,

Thank you so much ___(21)___ all the things
you do for me. To me, you are ___(22)___ mother
in the world. You are busy ___(23)___ the housework
day and night, but you never ___(24)___ the hard
work. ___(25)___ this special day, I wish you a happy
Mother's Day.

Love,
Sandy

21. A. to
    B. for
    C. with
    D. at

22. A. the most
    B. the worst
    C. the fewest
    D. the nicest

23. A. to do
    B. doing
    C. did
    D. do

24. A. show off
    B. be interested in
    C. be impressed by
    D. complain about

25. A. On
    B. At
    C. Of
    D. In

請 翻 頁 ⟹

第三部份： 閱讀理解

本部份共 10 題，包括數段短文，每段短文後有 1～3 個相關問題，請就試題冊上 A、B、C、D 四個選項中選出最適合者，標示在答案紙上。

Questions 26-27

WONDERLAND RESTAURANT

Dinner Specials

Soups	Corn Soup	$80
	Vegetable Soup	$70
Entrées	Steak	$260
	Lobster	$480
Dessert	Cheesecake	$45
	Lemon Pie	$30
Drinks	White Wine	$180
	Red Wine	$200
	Hot Coffee	$65
	Iced Tea	$55
	Pepsi	$35

參考上面的菜單，並且根據以下的對話回答問題。

Waitress : Good evening, sir. Are you ready to order now?

Michael : Yes, would you please give me a corn soup, and a lobster.

Waitress : Anything for dessert?

Michael : Lemon pie, please.

Waitress : Would you like anything to drink?

Michael : Hot coffee, please.

Waitress : Is that all?

Michael : How about some salad?

Waitress : Sorry, we don't have any salad.

Michael : That's OK.

Waitress : Anything else?

Michael : No, that's all.

26. What did Michael order for dinner?
   A. One corn soup and one steak.
   B. One lobster and one hot coffee.
   C. One white wine and one lobster.
   D. One vegetable soup and one salad.

27. How much did Michael spend on his dinner?
   A. $655
   B. $650
   C. $600
   D. $665

請 翻 頁 ||⟹

Questions 28-30

Most people have their own names, but not all people are given names in the same way.

In the United States, children have a family name and a first name. Most also have a middle name. Some people believe that those who have died will be born again as babies. Therefore, the parents name their babies by saying the names of their ancestors （祖先）. The baby may smile or cry when a certain name is said. The parents think that it means one of the ancestors is coming back, so the baby is given that name.

In some parts of Africa, a baby's name will not be told to strangers. That's because people there believe that the name is part of the child. They believe that strangers who know the name will be able to control the child.

28. What is true?
    A. People name children in different ways.
    B. People in Africa are afraid of giving names to babies.
    C. It's important to know a baby's name.
    D. It's true that our ancestors will come back as babies.

29. How do people who believe their ancestors will come back name their babies?

    A. They wait until the baby can give himself or herself a name.

    B. They write down a lot of names for the baby to choose from.

    C. They give the baby the same name as one of their ancestors.

    D. They ask their ancestors to name the baby.

30. What might happen if you went to some parts of Africa?

    A. You might have to give a baby a name.

    B. You might be able to control the baby.

    C. You could be given a baby.

    D. You might not know a baby's name.

請 翻 頁 ◗◖⟹

<u>Questions 31-32</u>

Dear Santa,

How are you? I know you're very busy, especially on Christmas Eve. But can you answer some questions for me? First, why do you always climb down into the house through the chimney? Why don't you knock on the door? If you ring the doorbell, I'll open the door for you. My older brother told me that you like good kids, so you only bring gifts for them. Is it true? If it's true, you owe me one. Mom always says that I'm the best girl that she's ever seen. But I didn't get any presents from you last Christmas. Please don't forget to bring a nice gift for me this year. ☺

Yours truly,

Rebecca

---

31. What does Rebecca suggest Santa Claus do?
    A. Climb down into the house through the chimney.
    B. Ride a bicycle.
    C. Ring the doorbell when he comes.
    D. Give her brother two gifts next year.

32. Which is **NOT** Rebecca's question?
    A. Can she be a Santa?
    B. Why does Santa always climb down into one's house through the chimney?
    C. Why didn't she get a gift last year?
    D. Why doesn't Santa knock on the door?

Question 33

33. What does this sign mean?
    A. You can park here.
    B. Be careful of people who cross here.
    C. You cannot turn right.
    D. Don't eat and drink here.

請翻頁 ⫘⟹

Questions 34-35

Shin-shin Movie Theater
The Ruby Hall
🎵🎵 Love On the Moon 🎵🎵
Line 7 No.7
91/11/20   7:40 P.M.
Adult: NT $250

34. When will the movie start?
    A. 7:40 A.M.
    B. 7:40 P.M.
    C. 11:20 A.M.
    D. 11:20 P.M.

35. How much is the movie ticket?
    A. NT $250.
    B. NT $150.
    C. NT $170.
    D. Free.

三、寫作能力測驗

本測驗共有兩部份，第一部份為單句寫作，第二部份為段落寫作。測驗時間為 40 分鐘。

第一部份： 單句寫作

請將答案寫在寫作能力測驗答案紙對應的題號旁，如有拼字、標點、大小寫之錯誤，將予扣分。

第 1～5 題： 句子改寫

請依題目之提示，將原句改寫成指定型式，並將改寫的句子完整地寫在答案紙上（包括提示之文字及標點符號）。

1. What color does Lily like the best?

   Please tell me _____.

2. Mr. and Mrs. Robinson usually go to the gym after work.

   Where _____?

3. Mother : Did you do the dishes?

   Peter : Oh, I forgot.

   Peter forgot _____.

4. To bring a dead man back to life is impossible.

   It's _____.

5. Put on your sweater. (…it…)

   _____.

請翻頁 ▭▭▭⟹

第 6～10 題：句子合併

　　　　　請依照題目指示，將兩句合併成一句，並將合併的句子
　　　　　完整地寫在答案紙上（包括提示之文字及標點符號）。

6. I go to the library.
   I return the books. (用 to)

   _____.

7. I will meet Sarah tonight.
   I'll give her the CD. (用 when)

   I'll give Sarah _____.

8. We can go on a picnic.
   The weather is nice. (用 as long as)

   We can _____.

9. Mary is very young.
   Mary cannot go to school. (用 too…to)

   _____.

10. I have a good friend.
    My good friend sings well. (用 who)

    _____.

第 11～15 題：重組

請將題目中所有提示字詞整合成一有意義的句子，並
將重組的句子完整地寫在答案紙上（包括提示之文字
及標點符號）。答案中必須使用所有提示字詞，且不
能隨意增加字詞，否則不予計分。

11. Mike _____.
his mother / to take out / helped / the garbage

12. Did _____?
have / cake/ dessert / for / you

13. Martha _____.
late / never /for /is / school

14. Wendy _____.
so / that / studies / gets / hard / she / grades / good

15. How _____?
coffee / would / like / you / your

請 翻 頁 ▌▌▶

第二部份： 段落寫作

題目： 昨天是媽媽的生日，請根據圖片內容寫一篇約 50 字的簡短
描述。

初級英語檢定測驗模擬試題詳解④

一、聽力測驗

第一部份

Look at the picture for question 1.

1. (**C**) What is the girl doing?
   A. She is watching TV.
   B. She is playing video games.
   C. She is talking on the phone.

   * *video game* 電動玩具　　*talk on the phone* 講電話

Look at the picture for question 2.

2. (**B**) Where is the dog?
   A. It is resting.
   B. It is under the bench.
   C. It is next to the bench.

   * rest〔rɛst〕v. 休息
   bench〔bɛntʃ〕n. 長椅　　*next to* 在～旁邊

Look at the picture for question 3.

3. (**B**) How many birds are there in the tree?
   A. Three.
   B. Four.
   C. Five.

   * *in the tree* 在樹上

Look at the picture for question 4.

4. (**A**) Which description matches the picture?

        A. The man wearing a cap is writing.

        B. The two men are looking at each other.

        C. There is a chair in front of the desk.

        * description〔dɪˈskrɪpʃən〕 *n.* 敘述
        match〔mætʃ〕 *v.* 符合   wear〔wɛr〕 *v.* 戴
        cap〔kæp〕 *n.* (無邊的) 帽子   ***look at*** 看
        each other 彼此   ***in front of*** 在～前面

Look at the picture for question 5.

5. (**C**) Where is the woman?

        A. She is at the post office.

        B. She is at the bank.

        C. She is at the doctor's office.

        * ***post office*** 郵局   bank〔bæŋk〕 *n.* 銀行
        office〔ˈɔfɪs〕 *n.* 辦公室；診療室

Look at the picture for question 6.

6. (**B**) What are they doing?

        A. They are setting the table.

        B. They are sitting at the dining table.

        C. They are drinking together.

        * ***set the table*** 擺餐具   ***sit at*** 坐在～前面
        dining table 餐桌   drink〔drɪŋk〕 *v.* 喝酒
        together〔təˈgɛðə〕 *adv.* 一起

Look at the picture for question 7.

7. (**A**)　What do you see in the picture?

　　　　A.　The woman is playing the piano.

　　　　B.　The piano is under the bench.

　　　　C.　Her feet are touching the keyboard.

　　　* piano〔pɪˈæno〕*n.* 鋼琴

　　　　foot〔fʊt〕*n.* 腳 (複數是 feet)

　　　　touch〔tʌtʃ〕*v.* 碰觸

　　　　keyboard〔ˈkiˌbord〕*n.* 鍵盤

Look at the picture for question 8.

8. (**A**)　What time will the store open?

　　　　A.　1:00 p.m.

　　　　B.　12:30 p.m.

　　　　C.　1:30 p.m.

　　　* store〔stor〕*n.* 商店　　open〔ˈopən〕*v.* 營業

　　　　p.m. 下午 (↔ *a.m.* 早上)

Look at the picture for question 9.

9. (**C**)　Where are they?

　　　　A.　They are in space suits.

　　　　B.　They are in spaceships.

　　　　C.　They are in space.

　　　* *space suit* 太空服

　　　　spaceship〔ˈspesˌʃɪp〕*n.* 太空船

　　　　space〔spes〕*n.* 太空

Look at the picture for question 10.

10. (**B**) What is going on?

      A. A bookstore has a sale.

      B. A library has a book sale.

      C. A library is for sale.

      * ***go on*** 發生 (= *happen*)

         bookstore〔'bʊk,stor〕*n.* 書店

         sale〔sel〕*n.* 拍賣

         library〔'laɪ,brɛrɪ〕*n.* 圖書館

         for sale 出售

第二部份

11. (**B**) What time do you leave for school?

      A. I get up at six o'clock on school days.

      B. About seven-thirty.

      C. I take the bus to school.

      * ***leave for*** 動身前往

         school days 求學時代

12. (**B**) How many people are there in your family?

      A. They are all fine, thank you.

      B. There are six, including me.

      C. My brother is older than I.

      * family〔'fæməlɪ〕*n.* 家庭

         including〔ɪn'kludɪŋ〕*prep.* 包括

13. (**C**) Where are you from?

    A. I came here by bus.

    B. I just came from the supermarket.

    C. Hualien is my hometown.

    * ***Where are you from?*** 你是哪裏人？

      supermarket〔'supɚ͵mɑrkɪt〕*n.* 超級市場

      Hualien〔'huɑ'lɪɛn〕*n.* 花蓮

      hometown〔'hom'taʊn〕*n.* 家鄉

14. (**C**) Do you want to go to the movies?

    A. I don't want to move to Taichung.

    B. That was a good movie.

    C. That's a good idea.

    * ***go to the movies*** 去看電影   move〔muv〕*v.* 搬家

      Taichung〔'taɪ'tʃʊŋ〕*n.* 台中

      idea〔aɪ'diə〕*n.* 主意；想法

15. (**A**) May I borrow your ruler?

    A. Here you are.   B. Thank you.

    C. It cost $100.

    * borrow〔'bɑro〕*v.* 借（入）   ruler〔'rulɚ〕*n.* 尺

      Here you are. 拿去吧。（= *Here you go.* = *Here it is.*）

      cost〔kɔst〕*v.* 值～（錢）（三態同形）

16. (**B**) Where did you go last Sunday?

    A. It was a holiday.   B. I went to the mountains.

    C. I don't go to school on Sundays.

    * holiday〔'hɑlə͵de〕*n.* 假日   mountain〔'maʊntn̩〕*n.* 山

      on Sundays 每週日（= *every Sunday*）

17. (**A**) Why did you go to the convenience store?

    A. I ran out of milk.   B. It was a nice day.

    C. I wanted to borrow a book.

    * ***convenience store*** 便利商店   ***run out of*** 用完
    nice〔naɪs〕*adj.* 美好的；天氣晴朗的

18. (**A**) Where should we have our picnic?

    A. How about the park?   B. Let's go before lunch.

    C. Let's go to McDonald's.

    * picnic〔'pɪknɪk〕*n.* 野餐
    How about~? ~如何？(= *What about~?*)

19. (**B**) How did you do on the geography test?

    A. I hope I can remember all the dates.

    B. I think I did pretty well.

    C. I forgot some important formulas.

    * geography〔dʒɪ'ɑgrəfɪ〕*n.* 地理
    remember〔rɪ'mɛmbɚ〕*v.* 記得   date〔det〕*n.* 日期
    do well 考得好   pretty〔'prɪtɪ〕*adv.* 很
    forget〔fɚ'gɛt〕*v.* 忘記
    important〔ɪm'pɔrtn̩t〕*adj.* 重要的
    formula〔'fɔrmjələ〕*n.* 公式

20. (**B**) Why didn't you come to school yesterday?

    A. It was too expensive.   B. I was sick.

    C. My boss gave me the day off.

    * expensive〔ɪk'spɛnsɪv〕*adj.* 昂貴的
    boss〔bɔs〕*n.* 老板   ***day off*** 放假

第三部份

21. (**B**) M: Where to, Madam?

W: The Regency Hotel, driver. How long will it take?

M: About thirty minutes. Traffic is heavy at this
time of day.

Question: Where does this conversation take place?

A. On a plane. 　　　　　B. In a taxi.

C. On the MRT.

* madam〔'mædəm〕 n. 女士
driver〔'draɪvɚ〕 n. 司機;駕駛人
take〔tek〕 v. 花費 (時間)　　traffic〔'træfɪk〕 n. 交通
heavy〔'hɛvɪ〕 adj. 繁忙的;擁擠的
conversation〔,kɑnvɚ'seʃən〕 n. 會話
take place 發生　　plane〔plen〕 n. 飛機
taxi〔'tæksɪ〕 n. 計程車　　**MRT** 捷運

22. (**C**) W: Attention, shoppers. The store will be closing in 15
minutes. Please bring your purchases to the nearest
register. Thank you for shopping at Macy's today.

Question: What should the shoppers do?

A. Go to Macy's today.　　　B. Close the store.

C. Pay for their purchases.

* attention〔ə'tɛnʃən〕 n. 注意
shopper〔'ʃɑpɚ〕 n. 顧客;買東西的人
close〔kloz〕 v. 關閉;停止營業
purchase〔'pɝtʃəs〕 n. 購買的東西
register〔'rɛdʒɪstɚ〕 n. 收銀機 (= *cash register*)
Macy's 梅西百貨公司　　***pay for*** 付錢買

23. (**C**) M：Today's weather will be partly cloudy with a chance of snow. Expect freezing temperatures today and tomorrow, but things should warm up by the end of the week, with a high of 5 °C.

Question：What season is it?

A. Spring.   B. Summer.

C. Winter.

* weather〔'wɛðɚ〕*n.* 天氣   partly〔'pɑrtlɪ〕*adv.* 部分地
cloudy〔'klaʊdɪ〕*adj.* 多雲的   chance〔tʃæns〕*n.* 機會
snow〔sno〕*n.* 雪   expect〔ɪk'spɛkt〕*v.* 預期
freezing〔'frizɪŋ〕*adj.* 嚴寒的
temperature〔'tɛmprətʃɚ〕*n.* 氣溫   **warm up** 回暖
by 表「在～之前」。   end〔ɛnd〕*n.* 結束
high〔haɪ〕*n.* 最高溫度   season〔'sizn〕*n.* 季節

24. (**B**) W：Can you tell me where I can find the Harry Potter books?

M：I'm sorry, but those books are out of stock. We should have more by the end of the week.

W：All right, then. I'll come back on Friday.

Question：What will the woman do on Friday?

A. She will call the bookstore.

B. She will buy the Harry Potter books.

C. She will visit Harry Potter.

* **Harry Potter** 哈利波特（書名）
out of stock 賣完了（＝*sold out*）   **come back** 回來
call〔kɔl〕*v.* 打電話給～   visit〔'vɪzɪt〕*v.* 拜訪

25. (**B**) M：Do you know where the bus station is?

W：I'm afraid I don't. I'm new here myself.

M：Thank you anyway.

Question：What is true about the woman?

A. She is afraid to go to the bus station.

B. She doesn't know where the bus station is.

C. She likes the new bus station.

* ***bus station*** 公車站　　***I'm afraid*** (*that*)~　恐怕~

new〔nju〕*adj.* 初到某地的

anyway〔'ɛnɪˌwe〕*adv.* 無論如何

true〔tru〕*adj.* 眞實的；正確的　　***be afraid to V.*** 害怕~

26. (**B**) W：What are you drinking? It smells terrible!

M：It's a new cold remedy. I have a sore throat.

W：Oh, I hope you get well soon.

Question：What is the man drinking?

A. He is drinking tea because he is cold.

B. He is taking medicine.

C. He is drinking a delicious cold drink.

* smell〔smɛl〕*v.* 聞起來　　terrible〔'tɛrəbḷ〕*adj.* 可怕的

cold〔kold〕*n.* 感冒　　remedy〔'rɛmədɪ〕*n.* 藥物；治療法

cold remedy 感冒藥　　sore〔sor〕*adj.* 疼痛的

throat〔θrot〕*n.* 喉嚨　　***sore throat*** 喉嚨痛

get well 康復　　***take medicine*** 吃藥

delicious〔dɪ'lɪʃəs〕*adj.* 好吃的　　***cold drink*** 冷飲

27. (**C**) W : What are you doing this weekend?

M : My friends and I are going to see a movie. Would you like to come?

W : I'd love to, but I can't. My grandmother will visit us this weekend and I should spend some time with her.

Question : What will the woman do this weekend?

A. She will take her grandmother to a movie.

B. She will see a movie with her friends.

C. She will keep her grandmother company.

* weekend ('wik'ɛnd) *n.* 週末
  go to see a movie 去看電影　　***would love to*** 想要
  grandmother ('grænd,mʌðɚ) *n.* 祖母；外婆
  spend (spɛnd) *v.* 花 (時間)
  company ('kʌmpənɪ) *n.* 同伴；陪伴
  keep sb. company 陪伴某人

28. (**A**) M : How about going on a picnic today?

W : That's a great idea. The weather is perfect in the mountains.

M : What kind of food should we bring?

W : Let's just pick up some fast food on the way.

Question : What will the man and the woman do?

A. They will eat their lunch outside in the mountains.

B. They will go out for lunch at a fast-food restaurant.

C. They will eat on the way to the mountains.

* ***go on a picnic*** 去野餐　　great (gret) *adj.* 很棒的
  idea (aɪ'diə) *n.* 點子　　perfect ('pɜfɪkt) *adj.* 完美的
  pick up 買　　***fast food*** 速食　　***on the way*** 在路上
  outside ('aʊt'saɪd) *adv.* 在戶外　　***go out*** 外出

29. (**A**) W：You look confused. What's the matter?

M：I can't find my history book, but I know I left it
on the table last night.

W：Then somebody must have moved it.

M：I'll ask Mom if she's seen it.

Question：Where did the man put his history book
last night?

A. He put it on the table.　　B. He gave it to his mother.

C. He moved it to a secret hiding-place.

* confused〔kən'fjuzd〕*adj.* 困惑的

What's the matter? 怎麼了？（= *What's wrong?*）

history〔'hɪstrɪ〕*n.* 歷史

leave〔liv〕*v.* 遺留　　then〔ðɛn〕*adv.* 那麼

must have + ***p.p.*** 過去一定～（表對過去的肯定推測）

move〔muv〕*v.* 移動　　if〔ɪf〕*conj.* 是否

put〔put〕*v.* 放置（三態同形）

secret〔'sikrɪt〕*adj.* 祕密的

hiding-place〔'haɪdɪŋ͵ples〕*n.* 隱藏處

30. (**A**) W：Please turn down the TV. I'm trying to sleep.

M：I'm sorry. I didn't realize what time it was.

Question：What did the man do?

A. He watched TV late at night.

B. He fell asleep while watching TV.

C. He told the woman what time it was.

* ***turn down*** 把聲音轉小（↔ *turn up*）

realize〔'rɪə͵laɪz〕*v.* 了解；知道　　late〔let〕*adv.* 晚

asleep〔ə'slip〕*adj.* 睡著的　　***fall asleep*** 睡著

二、閱讀能力測驗

第一部份：詞彙和結構

1. (**C**) Can I borrow your <u>cell phone</u> to make a call?
   我可以跟你借<u>手機</u>，打一通電話嗎？

   (A) dining room 餐廳　　(B) air conditioner 冷氣機

   (C) *cell phone* 手機　　(D) soft drink 不含酒精的飲料

   * *make a call* 打一通電話

2. (**D**) Whenever we sing in the KTV parlor, Sally always holds the microphone. I think she likes to <u>show off</u>.
   每當我們在 KTV 唱歌時，莎莉總是握著麥克風不放。我想她喜歡<u>炫燿</u>自己。

   (A) stay up 熬夜　　　　(B) get up 起床

   (C) give up 放棄　　　　(D) *show off* 炫燿

   * whenever〔hwɛn'ɛvɚ〕*conj.* 每當
   parlor〔'parlɚ〕*n.* 店　　hold〔hold〕*v.* 握著
   microphone〔'maɪkrə,fon〕*n.* 麥克風

3. (**D**) After eating the pizza, we asked the waiter for more <u>napkins</u> to wipe our oily hands. 我們吃完披薩後，向服務生再要一些<u>餐巾</u>，擦我們油膩的手。

   (A) menu〔'mɛnju〕*n.* 菜單

   (B) fork〔fɔrk〕*n.* 叉子　(C) glass〔glæs〕*n.* 玻璃杯

   (D) *napkin*〔'næpkɪn〕*n.* 餐巾紙

   * pizza〔'pitsə〕*n.* 披薩　　*ask sb. for sth.* 向某人要某物
   waiter〔'wetɚ〕*n.* 服務生　　wipe〔waɪp〕*v.* 擦
   oily〔'ɔɪlɪ〕*adj.* 油膩的

4. (**A**) Linda put on ten kilograms during the summer vacation, so she decided to go <u>on</u> a diet.

琳達在暑假期間胖了十公斤，所以她決定要<u>節食</u>。

　　go on a diet 節食

　　* ***put on*** 增加　　kilogram〔'kɪləˌgræm〕 n. 公斤 (= *kilo*)
　　during〔'djʊrɪŋ〕 prep. 在…期間
　　vacation〔ve'keʃən〕 n. 假期　　decide〔dɪ'saɪd〕 v. 決定

5. (**D**) George and Karen are afraid of their mother, because she is <u>strict</u> with them.

喬治和凱倫很怕他們的媽媽，因爲她對他們很<u>嚴格</u>。

　　(A) kind〔kaɪnd〕 adj. 親切的 < *to* >
　　(B) nice〔naɪs〕 adj. 好心的 < *to* >
　　(C) worried〔'wɝɪd〕 adj. 擔心的 < *about* >
　　(D) ***strict***〔strɪkt〕 adj. 嚴格的 < *with* >

　　* ***be afraid of*** 害怕

6. (**B**) The "thinking" car can slow down by itself if it is too <u>close</u> to the car in front.

會「思考」的車如果太<u>靠近</u>前面的車子，能夠自動減慢速度。

　　(A) quick〔kwɪk〕 adj. 快速的
　　(B) ***close***〔klos〕 adj. 接近的 < *to* >
　　(C) fast〔fæst〕 adj. 快速的
　　(D) direct〔də'rɛkt〕 adj. 直接的

　　* ***slow down*** 慢下來　　***by oneself*** 獨力；靠自己
　　in front 在前方

7. (**C**) The book was <u>so interesting</u> that the girl found it hard to put it down.

這本書<u>太有趣</u>了，所以這女孩覺得捨不得放下來。

> ***so⋯that~*** 如此⋯以致於~
>
> $\begin{cases} \text{interested} \ (\text{'ɪntrɪstɪd} \ ) \ \textit{adj.} \ (\text{人}) \ 感興趣的 \\ \text{interesting} \ (\text{'ɪntrɪstɪŋ} \ ) \ \textit{adj.} \ (\text{事物或人}) \ 有趣的 \end{cases}$
>
> 依句意，修飾 the book，故選 (C) ***so interesting***。

* find〔faɪnd〕*v.* 覺得   hard〔hɑrd〕*adj.* 困難的
  put down 放下

8. (**B**) Working overseas often <u>means</u> that you have to speak a foreign language.

到國外工作通常<u>意味著</u>，你必須會說一種外語。

> 動名詞當主詞視為單數，故選 (B) ***means***。

* overseas〔'ovɚ'siz〕*adv.* 在海外
  mean〔min〕*v.* 意思是   ***have to*** 必須
  foreign〔'fɔrɪn〕*adj.* 外國的
  language〔'læŋgwɪdʒ〕*n.* 語言

9. (**A**) Bruce is an American and has been in Taiwan for more than ten years. He can speak not <u>only</u> Chinese but also Taiwanese. 布魯斯是個美國人，他待在台灣超過十年了。
他<u>不僅</u>會說中文，也會說台語。

> ***not only⋯but also~*** 不僅⋯而且~

* American〔ə'mɛrɪkən〕*n.* 美國人
  Taiwanese〔,taɪwɑ'niz〕*n.* 台語

10. (**A**) Sandy and Sally are twins, but they are not like <u>each other</u>. 珊蒂和莎莉是雙胞胎，但是她們<u>彼此</u>不像。

    each other 互相

    而 (B) the other「（兩者中）另一個」，(C) another「（三者以上）另一個」，(D) both「兩者都」，均不合句意。

    * twins〔twɪnz〕*n. pl.* 雙胞胎   like〔laɪk〕*prep.* 像

11. (**B**) Please sit down and <u>read</u> the instructions carefully.
請坐下，並且仔細<u>閱讀</u>指示說明。

    and 為對等連接詞，故空格須填原形動詞，形成祈使句，故選 (B) ***read***。

    * instructions〔ɪn'strʌkʃənz〕*n. pl.* 指示；說明
carefully〔'kɛrfəlɪ〕*adv.* 仔細地；小心地

12. (**D**) My hair is darker than <u>hers</u>.
我的頭髮比<u>她的頭髮</u>黑。

    比較要以「對等的事物」做比較，故 (A) them 及 (B) your 不合，須改為 theirs 及 yours 才能選，而 (C) ours「我們的頭髮」，則不合句意。故選 (D) ***hers***，在此等於 her hair。

    * dark〔dɑrk〕*adj.* 黑色的

13. (**B**) What a wonderful winter vacation! We don't have <u>much</u> homework. 多麼棒的寒假啊！我們沒有<u>很多</u>功課。

    homework 是不可數名詞，可用 much 及 little 來修飾，且按照句意，選 (B) ***much***。

    * wonderful〔'wʌndəfəl〕*adj.* 很棒的

14. (**C**) Miss Li works in a fast-food restaurant in Taipei. She <u>has been</u> there since she graduated from senior high school. 李小姐在台北的一家速食店工作。她從高中畢業後，就在那裡了。

> 連接詞 since「自從」引導的副詞子句中，動詞時態用過去式動詞，而主要子句的動詞時態則用「現在完成式」，表示「從過去繼續到現在的動作或狀態」，故選 (C) *has been*。

* *fast-food restaurant* 速食店
graduate〔ˋgrædʒʊ,et〕*v.* 畢業 <*from* >
senior high school 高中

15. (**A**) <u>If</u> you see her, give her this important letter.
如果你看到她，把這封重要的信交給她。

> 依句意，選 (A) *If*「如果」。而 (B) Because「因為」，(C) So「所以」，(D) Although「雖然」，均不合句意。

* letter〔ˋlɛtɚ〕*n.* 信

第二部份：段落填空

Questions 16-20

We need our eyes to do a lot of things. Remember <u>to use</u>
16
enough light when you study at the desk. If you can't see <u>well</u>,
17
you should go to the eye doctor to have your eyes <u>examined</u>.
18
The doctor will write a <u>prescription</u> for you. Take it to a store and
19
buy <u>a good pair of glasses</u>.
20

　　我們需要眼睛去做很多事情。記得當你在書桌前閱讀時，要有充足的燈光。如果你看不太清楚的時候，就應該去看眼科醫生，檢查一下眼睛。醫師會開處方給你。帶著處方去眼鏡行，配一副適合的眼鏡。

> *a lot of* 許多　　remember〔rɪˋmɛmbɚ〕*v.* 記得
> light〔laɪt〕*n.* 光線　　*at the desk* 在書桌前
> *eye doctor* 眼科醫生　　*have* + *O.* + *p.p.* 使…被～

16. (**B**) remember 的用法是：

> remember + to V. 記得去（動作未完成）
> remember + V-ing 記得做過（動作已完成）

17. (**D**) *see well* 看得清楚（= *see clearly*）

18. (**D**) (A) clean〔klin〕*v.* 清洗
　　　　　　(B) celebrate〔ˋsɛləˌbret〕*v.* 慶祝
　　　　　　(C) change〔tʃendʒ〕*v.* 改變
　　　　　　(D) *examine*〔ɪgˋzæmɪn〕*v.* 檢查

19. (**C**) (A) letter〔ˋlɛtɚ〕*n.* 信；字母
　　　　　　(B) sentence〔ˋsɛntəns〕*n.* 句子
　　　　　　(C) *prescription*〔prɪˋskrɪpʃən〕*n.* 處方
　　　　　　(D) e-mail〔ˋiˌmel〕*n.* 電子郵件

20. (**A**) a pair of 表「一雙；一副」，而「眼鏡」一定要用複數形 glasses，故選 (A) *a good pair of glasses*（= *a pair of good glasses*）。而 (B) glass〔glæs〕*n.* 玻璃杯，(D) 時髦的玻璃杯，均不合句意。fashionable〔ˋfæʃənəbl̩〕*adj.* 時髦的

Questions 21-25

Dear Mom,

　　Thank you so much <u>for</u> all the things you do for
　　　　　　　　　　　 21
me. To me, you are <u>the nicest</u> mother in the world.
　　　　　　　　　　　　 22
You are busy <u>doing</u> the housework day and night, but
　　　　　　　 23
you never <u>complain about</u> the hard work. <u>On</u> this
　　　　　　　 24　　　　　　　　　　　 25
special day, I wish you a happy Mother's Day.

　　　　　　　　　　　　　　　　　　　　Love,
　　　　　　　　　　　　　　　　　　　　Sandy

親愛的媽媽：

　　感謝妳為我所做的一切。對我來說，妳是世界上最好
的母親。妳總是日夜不停地忙著做家事。但妳從不抱怨這
些辛苦的工作。在這特別的日子裡，我希望妳有個快樂的
母親節。

　　　　　　　　　　　　　　　　　　　　愛妳的，
　　　　　　　　　　　　　　　　　　　　珊蒂

---

in the world 在全世界　　housework〔'haʊs,wɝk〕*n.* 家事
day and night 日夜不停地　　hard〔hɑrd〕*adj.* 辛苦的
special〔'spɛʃəl〕*adj.* 特別的　　wish〔wɪʃ〕*v.* 祝福
Mother's Day 母親節

21. (**B**) *thank sb. for sth.* 感謝某人某事

22. (**D**) 依句意,「世上最好的母親」,故選 (D) *the nicest*。而 (A) 最多的,(B) 最差的,(C) 最少的,皆不合句意。

23. (**B**) *be busy + V-ing* 忙於~

24. (**D**) 依句意,妳從不「抱怨」,故選 (D) *complain about*,complain〔kəm'plen〕 v. 抱怨。而 (A) show off「炫燿」,(B) be interested in「對~有興趣」,(C) be impressed by「對~印象深刻」,皆不合句意。

25. (**A**) 「*on* + 特定日子」表「在(某日)」

第三部份:閱讀理解

Questions 26-27

奇境餐廳

晚餐特餐

湯	玉米濃湯	80 元
	蔬菜湯	70 元
主菜	牛排	260 元
	龍蝦	480 元
甜點	起士蛋糕	45 元
	檸檬派	30 元
飲料	白酒	180 元
	紅酒	200 元
	熱咖啡	65 元
	冰茶	55 元
	百事可樂	35 元

wonderland〔'wʌndə,lænd〕n. 奇境

special〔'spɛʃəl〕n. 特餐　　soup〔sup〕n. 湯

corn〔kɔrn〕n. 玉米　　vegetable〔'vɛdʒətəbḷ〕n. 蔬菜

entrée〔'antre〕n. 主菜（= main course）

steak〔stek〕n. 牛排　　lobster〔'lastə〕n. 龍蝦

dessert〔dɪ'zɝt〕n. 餐後甜點

cheesecake〔'tʃiz,kek〕n. 起士蛋糕

lemon〔'lɛmən〕n. 檸檬　　wine〔waɪn〕n. 葡萄酒

drink〔drɪŋk〕n. 飲料　　iced〔aɪst〕adj. 冰過的

參考上面的菜單，並且根據以下的對話回答問題。

Waitress : Good evening, sir. Are you ready to order now?

Michael : Yes, would you please give me a corn soup, and a lobster.

女服務生： 先生，晚安。您準備好要點餐了嗎？

麥　　可： 是的，請給我一份玉米濃湯和龍蝦。

Waitress : Anything for dessert?

Michael : Lemon pie, please.

女服務生： 餐後甜點要什麼呢？

麥　　可： 請給我檸檬派。

Waitress : Would you like anything to drink?

Michael : Hot coffee, please.

女服務生： 想要喝什麼飲料呢？

麥　　可： 請給我熱咖啡。

Waitress ： Is that all?

Michael ： How about some salad?

女服務生 ： 就這些了嗎？

麥　　可 ： 來些沙拉如何？

Waitress ： Sorry, we don't have any salad.

Michael ： That's OK.

女服務生 ： 很抱歉，我們沒有提供沙拉。

麥　　可 ： 沒關係。

Waitress ： Anything else?

Michael ： No, that's all.

女服務生 ： 還需要什麼嗎？

麥　　可 ： 不用了，就這樣。

waitress〔'wetrɪs〕n. 女服務生　　ready〔'rɛdɪ〕adj. 準備好的

order〔'ɔrdɚ〕v. 點餐　　***That's OK***. 沒關係。

salad〔'sæləd〕n. 沙拉　　***That's all***. 完畢；這樣就結束了。

26. (**B**) 麥可點了什麼當晚餐？

　　(A) 一份玉米濃湯和一份牛排。

　　(B) 一份龍蝦和一杯熱咖啡。

　　(C) 一杯白酒和一份龍蝦。

　　(D) 一份蔬菜湯和一份沙拉。

27. (**A**) 麥可的晚餐共花了多少錢？

　　　玉米湯（$80）＋龍蝦（$480）＋檸檬派（$30）

　　　＋熱咖啡（$65）＝ 655 元，故選 (A)。

Questions 28-30

Most people have their own names, but not all people are given names in the same way.

大部分的人都有自己的名字，但是並非所有的人都被以相同的方式來命名。

> way〔we〕n. 方式

In the United States, children have a family name and a first name. Most also have a middle name. Some people believe that those who have died will be born again as babies. Therefore, the parents name their babies by saying the names of their ancestors （祖先）. The baby may smile or cry when a certain name is said. The parents think that it means one of the ancestors is coming back, so the baby is given that name.

在美國，每個小孩有一個姓和一個名字。大部分的小孩還有中間名。有些人認為，已經過世的人會以嬰兒的方式重生。因此，父母親藉由說出祖先的名字來命名。在說到某個名字時，小嬰兒可能會微笑或哭。父母親認為這就表示有位祖先回來了，所以小嬰兒就以那個名字為名。

> *family name* 姓（= *last name*）
> *first name* 名（= *given name*）　　*middle name* 中間名
> believe〔bɪ'liv〕v. 相信；認為　　*be born* 出生
> as〔æz〕prep. 以⋯身份　　therefore〔'ðɛr͵for〕adv. 因此
> name〔nem〕v. 命名　　ancestor〔'ænsɛstɚ〕n. 祖先
> smile〔smaɪl〕v. 微笑　　certain〔'sɝtn̩〕adj. 某個
> *come back* 回來

In some parts of Africa, a baby's name will not be told to strangers. That's because people there believe that the name is part of the child. They believe that strangers who know the name will be able to control the child.

在非洲的某些地區,小嬰兒的名字不能告訴陌生人。那是因為那裡的人認為,名字是小孩的一部分。他們認為,知道小孩名字的陌生人,能夠控制那個小孩。

part〔part〕 *n.* 部分　　Africa〔'æfrɪkə〕 *n.* 非洲
stranger〔'strendʒɚ〕 *n.* 陌生人　　***be part of*** 是～的一部分
child〔tʃaɪld〕 *n.* 小孩　　***be able to*** 能夠
control〔kən'trol〕 *v.* 控制

28. (**A**) 何者為真?

(A) 人們以不同的方式為小孩命名。
(B) 非洲人害怕為小孩命名。
(C) 知道嬰兒的名字很重要。
(D) 我們的祖先真的會以嬰兒的方式重生。

* different〔'dɪfrənt〕 *adj.* 不同的

29. (**C**) 對於認為祖先會回來的人,他們會如何為嬰兒命名?

(A) 他們會等到嬰兒能夠為自己命名。
(B) 他們會寫下許多名字,讓嬰兒自己選擇。
(C) 他們會為嬰兒取和一位祖先相同的名字。
(D) 他們請祖先為嬰兒命名。

* until〔ən'tɪl〕 *conj.* 直到　　***write down*** 寫下來

30. (**D**) 如果你去非洲某些地區,可能會發生什麼事?

(A) 你可能必須為嬰兒命名。　(B) 你可能能夠控制嬰兒。
(C) 你可能獲得嬰兒。　　　　(D) 你可能不知道嬰兒的名字。

Questions 31-32

Dear Santa,

How are you? I know you're very busy, especially on Christmas Eve. But can you answer some questions for me? First, why do you always climb down into the house through the chimney? Why don't you knock on the door? If you ring the doorbell, I'll open the door for you. My older brother told me that you like good kids, so you only bring gifts for them. Is it true? If it's true, you owe me one. Mom always says that I'm the best girl that she's ever seen. But I didn't get any presents from you last Christmas. Please don't forget to bring a nice gift for me this year.☺

Yours truly,
Rebecca

親愛的聖誕老公公：

你好嗎？知道你非常的忙碌，特別是在聖誕夜。可是你可以回答我一些問題嗎？第一，你為什麼總是要從人家家裡的煙囪爬下來呢？你為什麼不敲門呢？如果你按門鈴，我會為你開門的。我哥哥說，你只喜歡乖小孩，所以你只送禮物給他們。這是真的嗎？如果這是真的的話，那你就欠我一份禮物。我媽媽總是說，我是她見過最乖的女孩。可是我去年聖誕節並沒有收到你的任何禮物。今年請不要忘了送我一份好禮物喔。☺

蕾蓓卡　敬上

Santa〔'sæntə〕*n.* 聖誕老公公（= *Santa Claus*）
especially〔ə'spɛʃəlɪ〕*adv.* 尤其是
first〔fɝst〕*adv.* 首先；第一點　　*climb down* 爬下來
through〔θru〕*prep.* 穿過；通過　　chimney〔'tʃɪmnɪ〕*n.* 煙囪
knock〔nɑk〕*v.* 敲　　ring〔rɪŋ〕*v.* 按（鈴）
doorbell〔'dor,bɛl〕*n.* 門鈴　　kid〔kɪd〕*n.* 小孩
gift〔gɪft〕*n.* 禮物（= *present*）　　owe〔o〕*v.* 欠
ever〔'ɛvɚ〕*adv.* 曾經　　last〔læst〕*adj.* 上一次的
yours truly 敬上（用於書信結尾）

31.（**C**）蕾蓓卡建議聖誕老公公做什麼？

　　(A) 從家裡的煙囪爬下來。　　(B) 騎腳踏車。

　　(C) 來的時候要按門鈴。　　(D) 明年給她哥哥兩份禮物。

32.（**A**）哪個不是蕾蓓卡的問題？

　　(A) 她能當聖誕老公公嗎？

　　(B) 為什麼聖誕老公公總是要從人家家裡的煙囪爬下來呢？

　　(C) 她為什麼去年沒有收到禮物？

　　(D) 為什麼聖誕老公公不敲門呢？

Question 33

33.（**C**）這個告示牌是什麼意思？

　　(A) 你可以在此停車。

　　(B) 要注意穿越此地的人。

　　(C) 你不能右轉。

　　(D) 不要在此地飲食。

　　* sign〔saɪn〕*n.* 告示牌
　　　park〔pɑrk〕*v.* 停車　　*be careful of* 小心；注意
　　　cross〔krɔs〕*v.* 穿越　　*turn right* 右轉

Questions 34-35

```
新新電影院
紅寶石廳
☾ ☾ 月亮上的戀愛 ☾ ☾
第七排七號
九一年十一月二十日　　晚上七點四十分
成人：新台幣二百五十元
```

theater〔ˋθɪətɚ〕n. 電影院　　ruby〔ˋrubɪ〕n. 紅寶石
hall〔hɔl〕n. 大廳　　moon〔mun〕n. 月亮
line〔laɪn〕n. 排　　**P.M.** 下午（↔ *A.M.*）
adult〔əˋdʌlt〕n. 成人

34.（ **B** ）電影何時開始？

　　(A) 早上七點四十分。　　　(B) <u>晚上七點四十分。</u>

　　(C) 早上十一點二十分。　　(D) 晚上十一點二十分。

　　* start〔stɑrt〕v. 開始

35.（ **A** ）電影票要多少錢？

　　(A) <u>新台幣二百五十元。</u>　　(B) 新台幣一百五十元。

　　(C) 新台幣一百七十元。　　(D) 免費。

　　* free〔fri〕*adj.* 免費的

三、寫作能力測驗

第一部份：單句寫作

第1~5題：句子改寫

1. What color does Lily like the best?

   Please tell me _____.

   > 重點結構：間接問句做名詞子句
   >
   > 　解　答：<u>Please tell me what color Lily likes the best.</u>
   >
   > 句型分析：Please tell me + what color + 主詞 + 動詞
   >
   > 　説　明：在 wh-問句前加 Please tell me，須改為間接問句，
   > 　　　　　 把動詞 like 放在主詞 Lily 的後面，又因主詞為第三
   > 　　　　　 人稱單數，like 須加 s，並把問號改成句點。
   >
   > * color〔ˈkʌlə〕*n.* 顏色

2. Mr. and Mrs. Robinson usually go to the gym after work.

   Where _____?

   > 重點結構：現在式的 wh-問句
   >
   > 　解　答：<u>Where do Mr. and Mrs. Robinson usually go</u>
   > 　　　　　 <u>after work?</u>
   >
   > 句型分析：Where + do + 主詞 + 動詞
   >
   > 　説　明：這一題應將現在式直述句改為 wh-問句，除了加助
   > 　　　　　 動詞 do，還要記得助動詞後面要用原形動詞 go。
   >
   > * gym〔dʒɪm〕*n.* 健身房　　***after work*** 下班後

3. Mother: Did you do the dishes?

   Peter : Oh, I forgot.

   Peter forgot _____.

   　　重點結構：「forget + to V.」的用法

   　　　解　答：<u>Peter forgot to do the dishes.</u>

   　　句型分析：主詞 + forget + to V.

   　　　説　明：「忘記去做某件事」用 forget + to V. 來表達，此
   　　　　　　　　題須在 forget 之後加不定詞。

   　　* **do the dishes** 洗碗

4. To bring a dead man back to life is impossible.

   It's _____.

   　　重點結構：以 It 爲虛主詞引出的句子

   　　　解　答：<u>It's impossible to bring a dead man back to life.</u>

   　　句型分析：It's + 形容詞 + to V.

   　　　説　明：虛主詞 It 代替不定詞片語，不定詞片語 to bring a
   　　　　　　　　dead man back to life 則擺在句尾。

   　　* **bring sb. back to life** 使某人復活　　dead〔dɛd〕*adj.* 死亡的
   　　　impossible〔ɪmˈpɑsəbḷ〕*adj.* 不可能的

5. Put on your sweater. (…it…)

   _____.

   　　重點結構：put on 的用法

   　　　解　答：<u>Put it on.</u>

句型分析：put + 代名詞 + on

説　明：put on「穿上」為可分片語，故「穿上毛衣。」有
兩種寫法，即 Put on your sweater. 或 Put your
sweater on. 若用代名詞 it 代替 your sweater，則只
能放在 put 跟 on 的中間。

第 6～10 題：句子合併

6. I go to the library.
I return the books. (用 to)

_____

重點結構：不定詞的用法

解　答：<u>I go to the library to return the books.</u>

句型分析：I go to the library + to V.

説　明：這題的意思是說「我去圖書館還書」。用不定詞
來合併兩句，不定詞在此表目的。

* return〔rɪ'tɝn〕v. 歸還

7. I will meet Sarah tonight.
I'll give her the CD. (用 when)
I'll give Sarah _____.

重點結構：未來式的 wh-子句

解　答：<u>I'll give Sarah the CD when I meet her tonight.</u>

句型分析：I'll give Sarah the CD + when + 主詞 + 動詞

説　明：在表時間的副詞子句中，要用現在式代替未來式，
所以雖然「我今晚會與 Sarah 會面」是未來的時間，
但不能寫成 when I _will meet_ Sarah tonight，須用
when I _meet_ Sarah tonight。

8. We can go on a picnic.

   The weather is nice. (用 as long as)

   We can ＿＿＿＿＿＿＿＿＿＿＿＿＿＿＿＿＿＿＿＿.

     重點結構：as long as 的用法

     解 答：<u>We can go on a picnic as long as the weather</u>
         <u>is nice.</u>

     句型分析：主詞 + 動詞 + as long as + 主詞 + 動詞

     說 明：這題的句意是「我們可以去野餐，只要天氣好的話」，
         as long as「只要」為連接詞片語，故後面要接完整
         的子句，即主詞加動詞的形式。

9. Mary is very young.

   Mary cannot go to school. (用 too…to)

   ＿＿＿＿＿＿＿＿＿＿＿＿＿＿＿＿＿＿＿＿＿＿.

     重點結構：「too + 形容詞 + to V.」的用法

     解 答：<u>Mary is too young to go to school.</u>

     句型分析：主詞 + be 動詞 + too + 形容詞 + to V.

     說 明：這題的意思是說「瑪麗年紀太小，還不能上學」，
         用 too…to V. 合併，表「太…以致於不～」。

10. I have a good friend.

    My good friend sings well. (用 who)

    ＿＿＿＿＿＿＿＿＿＿＿＿＿＿＿＿＿＿＿＿＿＿.

      重點結構：由 who 引導的形容詞子句

      解 答：<u>I have a good friend who sings well.</u>

句型分析：I have a good friend + who + 動詞

說　明：這題的意思是說「我有一位很會唱歌的朋友」，在
合併時，用 who 代替先行詞 a good friend，引導
形容詞子句。

第 11～15 題：重組

11. Mike _____?

his mother / to take out / helped / the garbage

重點結構：「help + *sb.* + to V.」的用法

解　答：Mike helped his mother to take out the garbage.

句型分析：help + 受詞 + 不定詞

說　明：這題的意思是「我幫媽媽倒垃圾」，help 的用法是
接受詞後，須接不定詞或原形動詞。

* *take out* 拿出去　　garbage〔'gɑrbɪdʒ〕*n.* 垃圾

12. Did _____?

have / cake / dessert / for / you

重點結構：一般過去式問句的用法

解　答：Did you have cake for dessert?

句型分析：Did + 主詞 + 原形動詞？

說　明：這題是說「你有吃蛋糕，作為餐後甜點嗎？」，
have 在此表示「吃」的意思。

* dessert〔dɪ'zʒt〕*n.* 餐後甜點

13. Martha _____.

　　late / never /for /is / school

　　　重點結構：never 的用法

　　　　解　答：Martha is never late for school.

　　　句型分析：主詞＋be 動詞＋never

　　　　説　明：never 為頻率副詞，須置於 be 動詞的後面。

　　　＊ late〔let〕adj. 遲到的

14. Wendy _____.

　　so / that / studies / gets / hard / she / grades / good

　　　重點結構：「so＋形容詞＋that 子句」的用法

　　　解　答：Wendy studies so hard that she gets good grades.

　　　句型分析：主詞＋動詞＋so＋副詞＋that＋主詞＋動詞

　　　　説　明：這題的意思是說「溫蒂非常用功唸書，所以她得到好
　　　　　　　　成績」，合併兩句時，用「so…that～」，表「如此
　　　　　　　　…以致於～」。

15. How _____?

　　coffee / would / like / you / your

　　　重點結構：wh-問句的用法

　　　　解　答：How would you like your coffee?

　　　句型分析：How＋助動詞＋主詞＋動詞

　　　　説　明：整句的意思是「你想要怎麼樣的咖啡？」，是問
　　　　　　　　人要不要加糖或奶精的說法。

第二部份：段落寫作

題目：昨天是媽媽的生日，請根據圖片內容寫一篇約 50 字的簡短
描述。

Yesterday was my mother's birthday. *In the morning* my brother and I went to a bakery. We bought a delicious cake. *In the afternoon* we went shopping for a present. We found a beautiful sweater. It was on sale, so it was not too expensive. *Last night* we all sang Happy Birthday to my mother. We had a wonderful birthday party.

bakery〔'bekərɪ〕*n.* 麵包店   *shop for ~* 去買～

present〔'prɛznt〕*n.* 禮物   sweater〔'swɛtə〕*n.* 毛衣

on sale 特價中   wonderful〔'wʌndəfəl〕*adj.* 很棒的

附錄

全民英語能力分級檢定測驗簡介

「全民英語能力分級檢定測驗」（General English Proficiency Test），簡稱「全民英檢」（GEPT），旨在提供我國各階段英語學習者一公平、可靠、具效度之英語能力評量工具，測驗對象包括在校學生及一般社會人士，可做為學習成果檢定、教學改進及公民營機構甄選人才等之參考。

本測驗為標準參照測驗（criterion-referenced test），參考當前我國英語教育體制，制定分級標準，整套系統共分五級——初級（Elementary）、中級（Intermediate）、中高級（High-Intermediate）、高級（Advanced）、優級（Superior）。每級訂有明確能力標準（詳見表一綜合能力說明），報考者可依英語能力選擇適當級數報考，每級均包含聽、說、讀、寫四項完整的測驗，通過所報考級數的能力標準即可取得該級的合格證書。各級命題設計均參考目前各階段英語教育之課程大綱及相關教材之內容分析，期能符合國內各階段英語教育的需求、反應本土的生活經驗與特色。

「全民英語能力檢定分級測驗」各級綜合能力說明　　《表一》

級數	綜　合　能　力	備	註
初級	通過初級測驗者具有基礎英語能力，能理解和使用淺易日常用語，英語能力相當於國中畢業者。	建議下列人員宜具有該級英語能力	一般行政助理、維修技術人員、百貨業、餐飲業、旅館業或觀光景點服務人員、計程車駕駛等。
中級	通過中級測驗者具有使用簡單英語進行日常生活溝通的能力，英語能力相當於高中職畢業者。		一般行政、業務、技術、銷售人員、護理人員、旅館、飯店接待人員、總機人員、警政人員、旅遊從業人員等。
中高級	通過中高級測驗者英語能力逐漸成熟，應用的領域擴大，雖有錯誤，但無礙溝通，英語能力相當於大學非英語主修系所畢業者。		商務、企劃人員、祕書、工程師、研究助理、空服人員、航空機師、航管人員、海關人員、導遊、外事警政人員、新聞從業人員、資訊管理人員等。

級數	綜　合　能　力	備		註
高級	通過高級測驗者英語流利順暢，僅有少許錯誤，應用能力擴及學術或專業領域，英語能力相當於國內大學英語主修系所或曾赴英語系國家大學或研究所進修並取得學位者。	建議下列人員宜具有該級英語能力	高級商務人員、協商談判人員、英語教學人員、研究人員、翻譯人員、外交人員、國際新聞從業人員等。	
優級	通過優級測驗者的英語能力接近受過高等教育之母語人士，各種場合均能使用適當策略作最有效的溝通。		專業翻譯人員、國際新聞特派人員、外交官員、協商談判主談人員等。	

初級英語能力測驗簡介

I. 通過初級檢定者的英語能力

聽	說	讀	寫
能聽懂簡易的英語句子、對話及故事。	能簡單地自我介紹並以簡易英語對答；能朗讀簡易文章。	能瞭解簡易英語對話、短文、故事及書信的內容；能看懂常用的標示。	能寫簡單的英語句子及段落。

II. 測　驗　內　容

測驗項目	初　試			複　試
	聽力測驗	閱讀能力測驗	寫作能力測驗	口說能力測驗
總題數	30	35	16	18
作答時間 / 分鐘	約 20	35	40	約 10
測驗內容	看圖辨義 問答 簡短對話	詞彙和結構 段落填空 閱讀理解	單句寫作 段落寫作	複誦 朗讀句子與短文 回答問題

聽力及閱讀能力測驗成績採標準計分方式，60 分爲平均數，滿分 120 分。寫作及口說能力測驗成績採整體式評分，使用級分制，分爲 0～5 級分，再轉換成百分制。各項成績通過標準如下：

III. 成績計算及通過標準

初　試	通過標準 / 滿分	複　試	通過標準 / 滿分
聽力測驗 閱讀能力測驗 寫作能力測驗	80 / 120 分 80 / 120 分 70 / 100 分	口說能力測驗	80 / 100 分

IV. 寫作能力測驗級分說明

第一部份：單句寫作級分說明

級　分	說　　明
2	正確無誤。
1	有誤，但重點結構正確。
0	錯誤過多、未答、等同未答。

第二部份：段落寫作級分說明

級　分	說　　明
5	正確表達題目之要求；文法、用字等幾乎無誤。
4	大致正確表達題目之要求；文法、用字等有誤，但不影響讀者之理解。
3	大致回答題目之要求，但未能完全達意；文法、用字等有誤，稍影響讀者之理解。
2	部份回答題目之要求，表達上有令人不解/誤解之處；文法、用字等皆有誤，讀者須耐心解讀。
1	僅回答1個問題或重點；文法、用字等錯誤過多，嚴重影響讀者之理解。
0	未答、等同未答。

各部份題型之題數、級分及總分計算公式：

分項測驗	測驗題型	各部份題數	每題級分	佔總分比重
第一部份：單句寫作	A. 句子改寫	5題	2分	50 %
	B. 句子合併	5題	2分	
	C. 重組	5題	2分	
第二部份：段落寫作	看圖表寫作	1篇	5分	50 %
總分計算公式	公式：{(第一部份得分/30)＋(第二部份得分/5)}×50 例：第一部份各項得分 A－8分 　　　　　　　　　　 B－10分 　　　　　　　　　　 C－8分 8+10+8=26 三項加總第一部份得分 － 26分 第二部份得分 － 4分 依公式計算如下： {(26/30)＋(4/5)}×50=83　該考生得分83分			

　　凡應考且合乎規定者一律發給成績單。初試及複試各項測驗成績通過者，發給合格證書，本測驗成績紀錄保存兩年。

　　初試通過者，可於一年內單獨報考複試，得重複報考。惟複試一旦通過，即不得再報考。

　　已通過本英檢測驗初級，一年內不得再報考同級數之測驗。違反本規定報考者，其應試資格將被取消，且不退費。

（以上資料取自「全民英檢學習網站」http://www.gept.org.tw）

劉毅英文國三基本學力測驗模考班

I. **招生對象：**全國國三學生

II. **開課班級：**

英文 A 班	每週六上午 9：00～12：00	自然 A 班	每週六下午 1：30～ 5：00
英文 B 班	每週六下午 2：00～ 5：00	自然 B 班	每週六晚上 6：00～ 9：30
英文 C 班	每週六晚上 6：00～ 9：00	自然資優班	每週日上午 9：00～12：30
英文 D 班	每週日上午 9：00～12：00	國文 A 班	每週日下午 1：30～ 5：00
英文資優班	每週六下午 2：00～ 5：00	國文 B 班	每週六晚上 6：00～ 9：30
數學 A 班	每週六上午 9：00～12：30	社會 A 班	每週日晚上 6：00～ 9：30
數學 B 班	每週日上午 9：00～12：30	社會 B 班	每週日晚上 6：00～ 9：30
數學資優班	每週日下午 1：30～ 5：00		

III. **獎學金制度：**

1. 本班同學在學校班上，國三上學期總成績，只要有一次第一名者，可獲得獎學金 *3000* 元，第二名 *1000* 元，第三名 *1000* 元。

2. 學校模擬考試，只要有一次班上前五名，可得獎學金 *1000* 元。

3. 每次來本班考模擬考試，考得好有獎，進步也有獎，各種獎勵很多。

IV. **授課內容：**

1. 本班獨創**模擬考制度**。
   根據「基本學力測驗」最新命題趨勢，蒐集命題委員參考資料，完全比照學力測驗題型編排。「基本學力測驗」得高分的秘訣，就是：**模擬考試➡上課檢討➡針對弱點加以加強**。

2. **本班掌握最新命題趨勢**：題型全為單一選擇題、題材以多樣化及實用性為原則。英文科加考書信、時刻表等題型；數學科則著重觀念題型，須建立基本觀念，融會貫通；理化科著重於實驗及原理運用。我們聘請知名高中學校老師（如建中、北一女、師大附中、中山、成功等），**完全按照基本學力測驗的題型命題**。

3. 每週上課前先考 50 分鐘模擬考，考後老師立即講解，馬上釐清同學錯誤的觀念。當天考卷改完，立即發還。

劉毅英文家教班（兒美、國中、高中、成人班、全民英檢代辦報名）
國中部：台北市重慶南路一段 10 號 7 F（消防隊斜對面）　　☎（02）2381-3148
高中部：台北市許昌街 17 號 6 F（壽德大樓）　　☎（02）2389-5212

劉毅專為國中同學設計的新資料

1. 　基本學力字彙 380 題　　（劉毅主編，售價 220 元）

　　由資深名師從國中英語第一冊至第五冊地毯式命題，每條題目的關鍵字均無重複，能幫助同學徹底複習國中單字。本書版面經特殊排版，同學一看就有想做題目的衝動。

2. 　基本學力閱讀測驗　　（張碧紋主編，售價 180 元）

　　本書出自大規模考試，每篇文章均附有翻譯，及單字註解，節省同學查字典的時間。內容豐富，完全符合考試趨勢，是國三同學提昇英文閱讀能力的最佳寶典。

3. 　國民中學基本學力測驗英語科模擬試題①②③④⑤⑥　　（劉毅主編，每冊 220 元）

　　本書為國三同學必備的應考利器，全新資料，符合考試趨勢。由知名高中資深英文老師命題，完全依照教育部「國民中學學生基本學力測驗英語練習題本」題型命題。

4. 　高中甄選入學第二階段測驗　　（張碧紋主編，售價 180 元，卡帶四卷 500 元）

　　本書完全根據建中、北一女、附中、成功、景美、松山、大同高中等校命題方向，編寫而成的模擬試題，含聽力及寫作測驗。聽力部分附錄音帶幫助讀者練習，並附有詳解。作文則附有範例，供讀者背誦。

5. 　基本學力克漏字測驗　　（張碧紋主編，售價 180 元）

　　本書完全符合大考中心「國民中學基本學力測驗」的命題方式，是每位國中生必備的參考書籍。書中每一回試題均附有翻譯及單字、片語的註釋，讓國三同學輕鬆征服克漏字。

6. 　初級英語聽力檢定①②③④　　（劉毅主編，書每冊 180 元，卡帶四卷 500 元）

　　本書為國三升高中「基本學力測驗第二階段考試」必備書籍，許多知名高中，如：北一女、建中、附中、中山女中、成功高中、景美女中等，均在第二階段甄試，加考聽力測驗。同學只要熟讀本書，一定可以高分通過。

7. 　基本學力文法 280 題　　（林銀姿主編，售價 180 元）

　　書中每條題目，都是從國內外大規模考試中整理出來，題題具代表性。每條題目都有詳解，並附有翻譯及註釋，讀完本書，英文文法實力立刻提升。

||||||||||||||● 學習出版公司門市部 ●||||||||||||||||

台北地區：台北市許昌街 10 號 2 樓　TEL：(02)2331-4060・2331-9209
台中地區：台中市綠川東街 32 號 8 樓 23 室
　　　　　 TEL：(04)2223-2838

||||||||||||||||||||||||||||||||||||||||||||||||

初級英檢模擬試題①

主　　　編／林銀姿
發 行 所／學習出版有限公司　　　☎ (02) 2704-5525
郵 撥 帳 號／0512727-2 學習出版社帳戶
登 記 證／局版台業 2179 號
印 刷 所／裕強彩色印刷有限公司
台 北 門 市／台北市許昌街 10 號 2 F　　☎ (02) 2331-4060・2331-9209
台 中 門 市／台中市綠川東街 32 號 8 F 23 室　☎ (04) 2223-2838
台灣總經銷／紅螞蟻圖書有限公司　　☎ (02) 2795-3656
美國總經銷／Evergreen Book Store　　☎ (818) 2813622
本公司網址　www.learnbook.com.tw
電 子 郵 件　learnbook@learnbook.com.tw

售價：新台幣二百二十元正

2006 年 11 月 1 日新修訂

ISBN 957-519-662-7